# GOBLINS
## IN THE CASTLE

Read the fantastical sequel to *Goblins in the Castle*:

*Goblins on the Prowl*

And don't forget these other Bruce Coville titles:

*My Teacher Is an Alien*
*My Teacher Fried My Brains*
*My Teacher Glows in the Dark*
*My Teacher Flunked the Planet*

# GOBLINS
## IN THE CASTLE

# BRUCE COVILLE

*Illustrated by Katherine Coville*

### Aladdin
New York  London  Toronto  Sydney  New Delhi

ALADDIN

An imprint of Simon & Schuster Children's Publishing Division
1230 Avenue of the Americas, New York, NY 10020
This Aladdin hardcover edition June 2015
Copyright © 1992 by Bruce Coville
Jacket illustration copyright © 2015 by Eric Deschamps
Interior illustrations by Katherine Coville
Also available in an Aladdin paperback edition.

For information about special discounts for bulk purchases, please contact
Simon & Schuster Special Sales at 1-866-506-1949
or business@simonandschuster.com.
The Simon & Schuster Speakers Bureau can bring authors to your live
event. For more information or to book an event contact the
Simon & Schuster Speakers Bureau at 1-866-248-3049
or visit our website at www.simonspeakers.com.
Jacket designed by Jessica Handelman
Interior designed by Hilary Zarycky
The text of this book was set in ITC New Baskerville Std.
Manufactured in the United States of America 0515 FFG
2 4 6 8 10 9 7 5 3 1
Library of Congress Control Number 2014947294
ISBN 978-1-4814-3900-8 (hc)
ISBN 978-0-671-72711-6 (pbk)
ISBN 978-1-4391-1239-7 (eBook)

*Special thanks to Steve Clorfeine for the necessary solitude,*
*and to Paula Danziger for the listening.*

*For Laura*

# CONTENTS

## CHAPTER ONE

# DISCOVERY IN THE DUNGEON

I was found on the drawbridge of Toad-in-a-Cage Castle on a cold December night. I was naked, they tell me, wrapped only in a blanket and tucked in a basket. If the Baron had not been out riding that night he would not have seen me, and I would have been buried beneath the snow by morning.

To the surprise of Hulda, his housekeeper, the Baron didn't send me away. Instead, he hired a nurse to come and take care of me.

I liked Nurse, despite her unusual fondness for toads. However when I was about five she fell into the moat and was eaten by something or other.

After that I pretty much took care of myself.

I had the run of the castle and could go anywhere I wanted—except the North Tower, which was always locked. Naturally, I wanted to know what was up there. But I learned early on not to ask about it. Questions upset people.

Not that there were many people to upset; only the Baron, Hulda, and Karl, the young man who tended the library.

I liked Karl. He was very smart, and when he had time he would give me lessons. However, this did not happen often, because caring for the library was a big job. (The Baron owned so many books he had had to knock out the walls between seven rooms to hold them all!)

Most of what I knew about the outside world came from the books Karl shared with me.

The library itself was my favorite place in the castle. Its floor was covered by a thick, soft carpet, its walls made of dark wood. Mazes of tall, book-crammed shelves filled the interior. The windows, which curved out from the side of the building, were twice as tall as a man; the huge velvet curtains that covered them used to be red and were still soft and warm. On cold days I liked to take a book and curl up on one of the sills. Wrapping a curtain around me like a blanket, I would alternate between reading and staring out at the distant village, the forest, the mountains.

I often wondered what it was like out there, beyond the castle walls that I had never left.

From one of the windows I could see the North Tower, which was shrouded in mist on even the sunniest of days.

One rainy evening in October Karl was repairing books, Hulda was sleeping, and the Baron was hidden away with one of the mysterious visitors that sometimes came to the castle gate. I was on my own, as usual. For some reason—perhaps because the voices that moaned along the hallway outside my room had been so loud the night before—I couldn't settle down to read.

I went to my room and played with Mervyn, the rat I had tamed the year before. When he ran off, I decided to go to bed. Slipping out of my clothes, I pulled on my nightshirt, then drew aside the curtain surrounding my bed and climbed beneath the covers.

I couldn't sleep.

A streak of lightning sizzled through the night. I liked to watch lightning, so I got up and sat by my window. But the lightning did not continue. After a while I grew tired of watching the thick drops splat against the glass and decided to go exploring. I had been exploring the castle for years and still hadn't discovered everything about it—partly because it was so huge, partly because it had so many secret passages and hidden rooms. These were what I looked for when I explored. To find them I pushed bricks, moved picture frames, and fiddled with the knobs carved in the mantelpieces of the fireplaces.

Lighting a candle, I went to my own fireplace, which was tall enough to stand in. I pushed a certain brick and the fireplace swung around, putting me in the passage behind it.

I had discovered this passage when I was only six. Once in it, I could get into any other room on my floor. But since it *was* my floor, since I was the only person living there, it didn't do me much good.

The worst thing about the secret passages was that they were so dark. When I first started exploring I had tried taking torches with me, but somehow the Baron always found out and told me not to. I understood why; some passages were lined with wood, or even drapes, and it would have been easy to start a fire in them. Finally I had started carrying candles. They didn't provide *much* light, but they were better than nothing, and the Baron never said anything about them.

About a hundred feet from my room a hidden stairway led to some secret rooms in the East Tower. Holding my candle before me, I made my way to the steps, then climbed three flights to a room dominated by a clock several feet taller than I am. I had seen this clock many times without ever really looking at it. But on this day I felt a hunch about it.

Opening the glass-paneled door, I put my hand inside. The wood behind the counterweights seemed solid. But when I climbed a chair and moved the hands of the clock to point straight up, as if it were midnight, I heard the familiar whisper of a sliding panel. The back of the clock had disappeared!

5

I jumped off the chair. Squeezing my way through the clock's door, I found myself in a narrow passage. Keeping one hand against the smooth, cool stones of the wall, I moved slowly forward. Even with the candle, I didn't notice the stairway going down until I put my foot on a spot that wasn't there.

The jolt knocked the breath out of me. Had I not been going slowly, I probably would have broken my neck falling down that stairwell, which stretched as far as I could see, no matter how high I lifted the candle.

I began to count as I walked. Fifty steps. A hundred steps. Two hundred steps. By now I must be down among the wine cellars.

Three hundred steps! I began to wish I had changed back into my clothes. The air was cool down here.

I had to be far past the wine cellars now, all the way to the dungeons. I shivered. I had never been to the dungeons before. In fact, I only knew they existed because Karl had told me about them, hinting that they held dark secrets.

Four hundred steps. Four hundred and fifty.

*How far into the earth does this stairway go?* I wondered as I neared the five hundredth step. But number five hundred was the end of it.

Keeping my left hand pressed against the wall, I moved slowly forward.

Fifteen paces brought me to a wooden door held together by thick iron crosspieces.

I could either turn back or open the door. Grasping the latch, which was enormous, I struggled to lift it without making any sound. It's hard to say why I felt a need to move so quietly. I was sure I was alone. But something about moving in the darkness inspires silence.

Besides, I liked to keep secrets.

When I managed to lift the latch the door swung open easily.

I saw a light flickering in the distance.

My heart began to beat more rapidly. *Who could possibly be down here?*

Again I thought about turning back. But my curiosity was driving me on, and I felt confident I could move so silently no one would know I was coming— though I don't think even then I really believed there was anyone there.

I started toward the light. Soon I could tell that it came from beyond a curve in the wall. As I continued forward I could see the outlines of the stones in the floor. The wall itself was damp and slightly chilly beneath my fingers. Even so, I pressed myself against it when I reached the curve. Inching my way forward, I saw the source of the light—a torch, stuck in a bracket.

To my astonishment, I also heard someone singing! The voice was little more than a low growl, but the tune was rollicking.

I could not make out the words.

I stopped and tried to talk myself into turning back. But in my whole life I had never met anyone besides Nurse, the Baron, Hulda, and Karl. I had to know who was down here.

Dropping to the floor, I set my candle down and began to creep forward. Beyond the torch an open door led to the source of the singing.

Closer I crept, closer still, until I had almost reached the door. I took a deep breath.

Slowly, ever so slowly, I poked my head around the corner.

# CHAPTER TWO

# IGOR

*"BOO!"*

I screamed and jumped into the air, then landed on the floor with a thump. My heart was pounding so hard I thought it would beat its way out of my chest, my hands trembling so violently I could not push myself off the floor.

About three feet away from me a strange-looking person rolled on the floor, shaking with laughter. His snorts echoed weirdly from the stone walls.

After a while the man (if man he was) caught his breath and pushed himself to a sitting position. He had huge, deep-set eyes and a balding head that glowed softly in the torchlight. His nose looked as if it had once been squashed, for it spread broadly across his face—most of which was covered by a huge black beard that hung halfway to his knees. A large hump rose from the upper right side of his back. He wore an old fur coat that reached almost to his feet, which were covered by battered boots laced with thick strips of leather.

Next to him lay a lumpy brown something.

Still chuckling, he pointed at me and said, "Good joke on you, boy!" His voice was low and gravelly.

I pushed myself to my knees. "Who are you?" I asked. "What are you doing here?"

The stranger stopped snorting. "Me Igor. *Igor!* Igor live here. Igor always live here."

"What do you mean 'always'? I've lived here for eleven years, and I've never seen you."

He smiled, displaying a set of crooked yellow teeth. "You are baby in this castle. Igor been here more than . . ." He stopped and began to count on his fingers. Finally he looked up and said, "More than six hundred years."

It was my turn to snort. "No one has lived anywhere for six hundred years. People die before they get that old."

Igor shrugged, causing his hump to shift like someone rolling under a blanket. "Igor done that before.

Not much fun." Grabbing one of the thick, rusty chains that hung from the wall, he pulled himself to his feet. The hump caused him to stoop, so he was only a little taller than me.

Reaching down, he picked up the brown something that had been lying beside him.

"What's that?" I asked, climbing to my feet as well.

"Igor's *bear*!" he replied, swinging it through the air and whacking me on the head.

"Hey!" I yelled, expecting it to hurt. It didn't. Whatever this bear was, it was soft.

"See?" said Igor proudly. "Bear good for bopping."

"Can I look at it?" I asked, holding out my hands.

Igor stared at me. "No bopping!" he warned.

I shook my head. "No bopping," I promised, not bothering to add that I would have been terrified of trying to bop him.

Igor handed me the bear. I had never seen anything like it. Between two and three feet high, it was made of fur sewn together with crude stitches and stuffed with something soft. It was like a doll, only shaped like a bear instead of a human.

"Where did you get this?"

"Made it," said Igor, reaching out to take it back. I let go reluctantly. The bear was nice to hold.

Tucking the bear under his arm, Igor moved a few steps away. His left boot was twisted sideways, and it dragged behind him, giving him an odd, shuffling gait.

"How did you get here?" I asked.

"Igor always been here," he said with another of those shrugs. "This Igor's home."

"Surely you weren't born here."

"Born?" Igor wrinkled his brow as if he didn't understand. Then he smiled. "Oh, *born*. No, Igor not born here. Don't think Igor was born. Igor just *is*. Igor just *here*."

Clearly I wasn't going to get anywhere with this line of questioning. "Where do you get your food?" I asked.

"Take it."

I don't know what prompted me to get indignant about that, but I did. "I think I had better tell the Baron about you," I said. "You live in his castle without his knowing. You steal his food. He's not going to like this."

I regretted the remark the moment I made it. For one thing, the Baron could spare the food. For another, Igor swung to face me with a look that made me want to melt into the stones of the floor.

"Stupid boy!" he cried, shaking his bear at me. "You not tell Baron. Not tell anyone—or Igor fix you good."

I shivered.

"Igor got to eat," he continued in a voice like a growl. "Igor got to live. Igor live here. Only food in dungeon is mushrooms and little critters. Igor need more than that, so Igor take food. *That part of the deal!*"

"What deal?"

"Igor got job. Igor do job, Igor get food."

"What is your job?"

"Igor watch things."

"What things?"

He put a crooked finger to his lips and shook his head. "Old Baron say, 'Igor, if you know what good for you, keep your mouth shut.' Igor know what good for Igor. Igor keep mouth shut. Boy keep mouth shut, too, if boy know what good for *him*."

"My name William . . . *is* William," I said, inching my way toward the door. "And I won't tell anyone about you. I promise."

"Wait," said Igor. "Don't go. Stay and talk to Igor." He put his face close to mine and grinned. "Igor like talking to William."

Though he scared me, I liked talking to Igor, too. I had almost convinced myself to stay when he got an odd look on his face. Furrowing his brow, he whispered, "William hear that?"

I listened and felt a chill. Something was moving in the darkness beyond Igor's cell.

"Go, William!" he cried. "Go now! Run fast. Come back later."

"Wait," I said. "What's going on? Will you be all right?"

"Go!" cried Igor. "This Igor's job. William go! Now!"

Without waiting to see if I had done as he commanded he went shuffling down the corridor, dragging his bear by a back leg.

Soon he had disappeared in the darkness.

## CHAPTER THREE

# NIGHT NOISES

I stood for a moment, trying to decide what to do. Though I barely knew Igor, I felt that if he was in trouble I should try to help. On the other hand, he hadn't acted frightened so much as agitated.

What had made the noise? The sound was different from the moans and cries that so often disturbed my sleep upstairs. This sound was more . . . solid.

Holding my breath, I listened. I could hear Igor, a fair distance away now, still thumping down the hall. His footsteps stopped. A door creaked open.

Then his voice came thundering out of the darkness.

"William go. *Now!*"

I turned and ran, stopping only to retrieve my candle.

As I rounded the curve beyond his cell I heard Igor's voice, faint now, call, "Go now, but come back soon!"

I trudged up the five hundred steps to the East Tower, considering telling the Baron, or even Hulda or Karl, about Igor.

I didn't.

For one thing, Igor had asked me not to. For another, it was easy to *not* say things in that castle—especially things you weren't sure you wanted to say. After all, it was practically impossible to get the Baron's attention; he hardly knew I existed. Karl was always absorbed in his own work. And as for Hulda—well, Hulda couldn't hear much better than the bread dough she was kneading when I went to see her the next day. I would have had to shout at the top of my lungs to tell her about Igor.

It's one thing to whisper a secret, something else altogether to scream it out.

"Don't you be picking at that dough, William," Hulda bellowed as I stood watching her, trying to decide whether or not to say something about Igor.

She didn't shout out of anger. She always shouted, because of her bad hearing. It had been a relief to me when I finally figured that out; for years I had thought that she was permanently mad at me.

Knowing she wasn't serious, I darted my fingers into the floury mass being pounded beneath her plump hands and snitched a blob of dough.

"Do that again," she shouted, "and Granny Pinchbottom will come tweak your cheeks while you sleep!"

I made a face. Hulda had been telling me Granny Pinchbottom stories for as long as I could remember—grisly tales about an ugly old woman who liked to punish naughty children. The story that had frightened me most was about Hulda's finger. She had told it to me one morning when she caught me sticking my own finger into the sweet jar.

"See this!" she had roared, holding her right hand before my face. The tip of her index finger had been cut off just in front of the knuckle. The flesh where it had healed over was smooth and shiny.

I nodded and stared. I had long been both frightened and fascinated by the shortened digit.

"Granny Pinchbottom did that! I stuck this finger where it didn't belong one time too many, even though my mother told me not to. One morning I woke up and . . ."

She had trailed off, shaking the short finger before my eyes by way of warning. I was six at the time, and the story had so terrified me that I stayed away from the sweet jar—and anything else that might possibly fall into the category of "things I shouldn't touch"— for a week.

After a while Karl noticed my odd behavior. It took him a while to draw the story out of me. When I finally confessed my fear of Granny Pinchbottom he looked angry. "Listen, William," he said firmly, "there is no Granny Pinchbottom. She's just a character the old women in the village use to scare children into behaving."

"Are you sure?"

He had laid one hand on the thick leather-bound book at his side. "I'm sure. When I was little my mother and my aunts terrified *me* with stories of Granny Pinchbottom. Finally my father got sick of seeing me so frightened and took me aside to tell me the truth."

I smiled in relief. Karl smiled back—a rare event.

"Not that I would go sticking my finger in the sweet jar if I were you," he had added. "Who needs to be afraid of Granny Pinchbottom when you have Hulda to keep you in line?" Then he had tugged a strand of my butter-yellow hair and said, "Now scat! I have work to do."

That was what he always did when he wanted to get rid of me.

Though I thought about it every day, nearly a week passed before I made another visit to Igor. It was the night noises that finally prompted me to descend the five hundred steps again. They were growing louder, and I was finding it harder and harder to sleep.

It happened the fifth night after I met Igor. The noises were worse than I could ever remember. I pulled my pillow over my head but I could still hear them. To make things worse, I was restless myself. I felt as if there was something I should do. Only I couldn't figure out what it was.

Finally I pulled aside the curtains that surrounded my bed, climbed out, and began to pace around my room. Moonlight streamed through my window.

I stopped in front of the fireplace. I had always seen it as a way out. Suddenly I realized it was also a way *in*. That had never mattered when I thought there were only four of us in the castle. But if Igor had been living in the dungeons all these years, it must be possible that *other* people—or things—lived in the castle, too.

I went to my door. The moans and sighs seemed closer than usual. I began to have an odd feeling that there was some sense underneath them—as if they were not merely sounds, but some word trying desperately to be formed.

That was when I decided to visit Igor. If he had really lived in the castle for as long as he said, maybe he could tell me something about these midnight moans. Slipping into my clothes, I lit a candle. Then I pushed the brick that opened my fireplace and climbed the three flights to the East Tower. Moving the hands of the clock to midnight, I stepped through and began the long journey to the dungeon.

When I arrived at Igor's cell, the torch was burning outside the door. But Igor was nowhere to be seen.

It was the middle of the night. Where could he be?

I hesitated for a bit, then entered. I had come too far to just turn and go. Besides, I was tired, and it was going to be a lot harder going back up all those stairs than it had been coming down.

As I looked around the cell the first thing that caught my eye was a crude wooden shelf on which sat a number of oddly shaped objects. When I stepped closer I realized that they were carvings, some made from wood, others from stone. They were rough, not smooth and polished like the strange statues that stood in some of the rooms above. Nonetheless, they were fascinating. At first I thought they were supposed to be animals. Then I realized that though they had some animal-like details—a pig snout here, a toad face there—they represented something else altogether; something strangely human-like.

I became so engrossed in examining the carvings I didn't realize someone else had entered the room until a creaky voice said, "Put that down, or I'll turn you into a toad!"

I was so startled that rather than putting the carving down I threw it into the air.

## CHAPTER FOUR

# "THE MOST DANGEROUS NIGHT"

To my astonishment, the carving didn't fall. It simply hung in the air before my face.

"Unless you want four legs and a lot of warts, set it down carefully," said the intruder.

His warning was made particularly chilling by the fact that the carving I had been studying bore a strong resemblance to a toad. I glanced at it again and wondered if it had once been a person. Moving delicately, I returned it to the shelf.

Then I turned around.

The man facing me was even taller than Karl. He wore an old white robe cinched at the waist and leaned on a knobby staff. A few strands of wispy white hair straggled over his forehead, and a thin white beard sprouted from his chin. His nose was long, his eyes a strangely intense blue.

"Who are you?" I asked nervously.

"My name is Ishmael. But don't call me that."

"Then what should I call you?"

"Don't call me anything!" he cried, pounding his stick against the floor. "Who are you? Where is Igor?"

"I don't know."

Ishmael looked startled. "You don't know who you are?"

"No, I don't know where Igor is. I came to visit him, but he wasn't here."

The man's look turned to one of anger. "What did you do with him?"

"I didn't do anything with him!"

"Of course he didn't, you old fool," cried Ishmael, striking himself on the forehead.

I wondered why he was calling me an old fool until I realized he was talking to himself. Shifting his walking stick to his left hand, he leaned forward and said, "Listen . . . what did you say your name was?"

"I didn't."

"Didn't what?"

"Say what my name was."

"Well, what is it?"

"William."

"All right, listen, *William*—I want you to give Igor a message for me."

"What is it?"

"What's what?"

"The message!" I snapped, forgetting my fear in my impatience. "What do you want me to tell him?"

"Who?"

*"Igor!"*

The man looked startled. "Igor? Is he here? That's who I want to talk to."

I sighed. "No. He's not here. That's why you wanted me to give him a message."

"Right! Thank you for offering." He peered from side to side, as if a spy might be lurking in any corner, then leaned his bony frame down so he could look straight into my eyes and whispered, "Tell him the most dangerous night is almost here!"

A shiver tingled down my spine. "What does that mean?"

"Don't ask. Just give Igor the message!"

Ishmael straightened, slammed the base of his staff against the floor, and shouted a word I couldn't understand. A flash of light filled the little cell, and he vanished in the center of it. A moment later I heard his voice, as if from a great distance, exclaim, "Wow, that *hurt!*"

My mouth was hanging open in astonishment—and fear. Clearly a few of the buttons in Ishmael's brain had come undone. But if he could vanish in a puff of smoke like that, maybe he could really turn someone into a toad, too.

I waved my hand to clear the smoke and hoped Igor would be back soon. Crazy as Ishmael had been, this didn't seem like the kind of message that could be ignored. I would have written it down, if not for two problems: I didn't have anything to write with, and I had no idea whether or not Igor could read. So I had to stay until he returned.

I looked around the cell again. I didn't feel safe picking up any of the little carvings; Ishmael might decide he had forgotten something, show up in a flash of light, and turn me into a toad for having my hands on them. But the cell didn't have much else to look at, the only other items being a leather bag in the corner, a stack of unlit torches, a stone table and bench, and a pile of rags that I finally realized must be where Igor slept. It looked uncomfortable, and I felt a little sad to see it.

I plopped down on the stone bench. It didn't just

*look* uncomfortable, it was uncomfortable. After a few minutes I got up and walked around the cell again. Where was Igor?

I wandered back into the corridor.

No sign of him, no clue as to where he might be.

After a while I lifted the torch from the bracket that held it into the wall and began to walk in the direction Igor had gone the last time I was down here.

I passed several doors. I tried to open the first three, but they were locked. At the fourth I stood on tiptoe and tried to peek through the bars of the tiny window. I was not able to see anything, but for a moment I thought I could hear something moving. I started to call out, then thought better of it.

Suddenly I heard another noise. It wasn't like the moans upstairs nor the more solid sounds I had heard the last time I was down here. This sound was light, almost tinkling. I walked a bit farther and realized it was made by running water.

Intrigued, I began to walk faster. Soon I reached a place where the floor disappeared in a gap two or three times wider than I was tall. A narrow stone bridge spanned the gap; about ten feet beneath the bridge flowed a dark stream.

A set of stone steps beside the bridge led to the

water's edge. After a moment's hesitation I walked down them. A narrow, rocky ledge bordered the stream. To my right it led to solid stone wall, from beneath which flowed the stream. To my left—the direction in which the stream was running—was a tunnel. Ledge, stream, and tunnel extended in that direction as far as I could see by the torch's flickering light.

I dipped my fingers into the water. Cold. I raised a tiny handful to my lips. It tasted fresh and clear. Was this where Igor got his water? I wondered if he used it for his sewer as well. Stretching the torch over the water, I saw sinuous shapes swimming beneath the surface.

I considered following the ledge along the stream for a while but decided to turn back. I didn't want to miss Igor if he returned.

But when I got back to the cell it was still empty. I was restless and tired, and I wanted to go back upstairs. I felt myself growing sleepy and wished Igor would come back so I could deliver Ishmael's message. Finally I lay down on the pile of rags. Within moments I was sound asleep.

I was woken by a voice in the corridor growling:

Bop, bop, bop!
Bop them on their top!

Knock them on the head
When they fall down dead
Igor gets his bread!
Bop, bop, bop, bop, bop, bop, *bop*!

As the voice came closer I realized that what I heard wasn't growling, it was singing. More specifically, it was Igor singing. I was glad he was back—until I suddenly wondered if he might be angry that I had been in his cell while he was gone.

A surge of panic gripped me. It was too late to run into the corridor and try to pretend that I was just arriving. Desperate, I burrowed under the rags that made up Igor's bed.

## CHAPTER FIVE

# THE NORTH TOWER

Do you know what it feels like to realize you've done something truly stupid? Then you know how I felt about five seconds after Igor entered the room. It was impossible for me to get out of the room without his noticing me. If I had just stood there, he might have been angry, but at least I wouldn't have looked as if I had something to hide, as if I had been caught snooping.

Suddenly I had an idea. Waiting until Igor turned away from me, I jumped out from the rags and screamed *"Boo!"* at the top of my lungs.

*"Aiieee!"* cried Igor. Spinning around, he hit me over the head with the bear. Though the bear was soft, the force of the blow knocked me over.

29

"William!" cried Igor when he saw that it was me. "What you doing here?"

"I came to talk to you," I said, pushing myself to a sitting position.

"Why you scare Igor?"

"Because you scared me," I said, not bothering to add that I had also wanted to draw his attention away from the fact that I was hiding in his bed.

Igor looked puzzled. Then he looked mad, which was pretty frightening. Then he began to laugh. "Good joke on Igor! Igor scare boy. Boy scare Igor! Brave boy to scare Igor."

The way he said "brave" made me wonder what he would have done if he *hadn't* liked the joke.

"Listen, Igor, I have a message for you. Someone named Ishmael—"

"Don't call him that!"

I paused, then started again. "A *strange person* asked me to tell you, 'The most dangerous night is almost here.'"

Igor furrowed his brow. "Sound important."

"What does it mean?"

"Igor not know. Igor should know, but Igor forget. Sometimes things get foggy in Igor's head."

"Like the North Tower," I said.

Igor looked at me with fear in his eyes. "What about North Tower?" he asked nervously.

"Well, it has fog around it all the time, and I can't figure out what's inside it. So it's a lot like your head," I added, amused at my own cleverness.

"North Tower," muttered Igor, ignoring my joke. "Igor don't like North Tower."

"Why not?" I asked, serious now.

He was silent for so long I began to wonder whether he had heard me. When I looked at him I saw that his eyes had gone funny and far-away-looking, almost as if he were in a trance. I reached out and shook his arm. "Igor! Are you all right?"

He blinked. "William! Don't you know when someone thinking? Now you made Igor forget."

He made one of his humpy shrugs. "Something important up there," he said. "Something very important, and very not good. Igor remember that now. Igor remember that very most long time ago that tower got locked so it would stay locked forever. Something fierce and bad up there. But Igor don't know what it is. Igor can't remember."

He sounded as if he was starting to get angry, so I changed the subject. But his reaction made me more curious than ever about what was in that tower. Which reminded me of my original reason for coming down to visit him. "What about the noises?" I asked. "Do you know what causes them?"

"What noises?"

"The noises I hear at night. They're like moans, mostly—as if someone is very, very sad. Or a lot of someones. But I can never find them."

"Could be ghosts," said Igor, giving his bear a little squeeze.

"Did you ever see a ghost?" I asked.

"Don't think so. Hard to tell down here."

"Sometimes the noises keep me from going to sleep," I said. "That's why I came to see you tonight. The noises were keeping me awake, and I wanted to ask you about them."

As I spoke I found myself stifling a yawn.

Igor looked at me for a moment. "Here," he said at last. "Hold bear. Bear good for sleeping."

I woke in my own bed. I was confused at first. How had I gotten there? Then I began to have foggy memories of Igor guiding me up the long stairway from the dungeons. I had been stumbling with exhaustion. Finally Igor had just picked me up. Cradled in his arms, I had collapsed into a deep sleep.

I was wondering how Igor had known where to bring me when I was distracted by something moving under the covers. It was Mervyn. He climbed onto my pillow and stared at me, his whiskers twitching expectantly.

"If you want breakfast, you'll have to wait until I get some myself," I said, tapping him on the head with my finger.

Climbing out of bed, I shook myself out of my clothes, which were fairly filthy after the past night's adventures. Later I would take them down to the room where Hulda kept the washtubs. She didn't do laundry very often—once every several weeks at most. But I had plenty of clothes, and if I ran out, I could always find more in one of the abandoned rooms.

"You look tired this morning," shouted Hulda when I stumbled into the kitchen fifteen minutes later.

"I didn't sleep well last night," I said as she scooped up a bowl of porridge and handed it to me.

I took my usual place at the big table in the center of the kitchen and sliced a thick slab from the loaf of dark bread Hulda placed in front of me.

Though it had been years since I had raised the topic of the North Tower with anyone upstairs, Igor's strange reaction to my mention of it the previous night had made me curious. I decided to try asking Hulda about it.

"Lands' sakes, William," she bellowed, wiping her plump hands on her apron and brushing back a wisp of gray hair. "What do you want to ask a question like that for? Anything in this castle that's locked is probably locked for a reason. My guess is that tower went so long without anyone cleaning it that the Baron decided it was easier to lock the door and forget it than to take care of the mess. After all, the last housekeeper didn't take care of this place the way I do."

I resisted an urge to snort. I had been writing my name in the dust in various places around the castle since Karl had first taught me how over six years earlier. As far as I knew, the only signatures that no longer existed were the ones that had been covered by new dust.

Fortunately, Hulda's cooking was better than her cleaning. Slicing another piece of bread, I ate half and tucked the other half in my shirt to share with Mervyn later. On impulse I cut another slab and slipped that into my shirt as well. Maybe Igor would like it.

After I had taken Mervyn his breakfast I climbed the South Tower. I studied the countryside for a moment. It was brilliant with late October foliage.

Next I turned my gaze on the North Tower.

As always, it was swathed in a thick mist.

What was in there?

I decided to ask Karl.

The library was pleasantly warm that morning, with big fires burning in the huge stone fireplaces at either end. Weak autumn sunlight streamed through the windows, making puddles of light on the old carpet. The Baron sat at his desk studying a huge book with yellowed pages. "Morning, Jasper," he muttered as I walked past.

"Good morning, sir," I said, annoyed that, as usual, he had forgotten my name.

Karl sat at the far end of the library repairing the binding of an old book.

"How are you today, William?" he asked when I walked up.

"Just fine," I replied. I watched him for a moment, admiring the way his long fingers could work the glue and the leather to make the repair mark almost invisible. When he was finished I said, "Karl, why is the North Tower locked?"

His fingers slipped, making a botch of the careful work he had just done. He didn't seem to notice. "Why do you want to know?" His voice was low, almost a hiss.

"Well, it's the only place in the castle I can't go. There must be some reason."

"I'm sure there is," said Karl, his voice even lower than before. "But I don't know what it is. And I wouldn't ask *him* if I were you," he added, gesturing toward the Baron with a nod of his head. "I asked once, and it almost cost me my job. It's something we don't talk about. I'll say this, though: Anything in this castle that's locked probably has good reason to be. So I wouldn't go messing with it if I were you."

"But—"

"That's all I have to say about it!" snapped Karl.

I turned and walked away, puzzled and angry.

I decided it was time to go see Igor. The trip was easier now that I had made it a couple of times, and it seemed to take less time to reach his cell.

"William!" he cried joyfully when he saw me at the door. "Glad you here!"

"I brought something for you," I said, reaching into my shirt and taking out the slab of bread I had saved for him.

Igor's eyes lit up. "Food!" he cried, reaching for it. Snatching the bread from my fingers, he turned and began to stuff it into his face.

"I'm glad you like it," I said, surprised and amused

by his reaction. Feeling a sudden fondness for Igor, who might have been odder than anyone else in the castle but was at least willing to talk to me, I patted him on the back.

"Don't do that!" he screamed, spinning around and staring at me with a look of anger so intense it made me fear for my life. His fists were clenched, and he was trembling with rage.

I shrank against the wall, well aware that he could tear me limb from limb if he wanted.

He started toward me.

## CHAPTER SIX

# THE TOWER DOOR

"Igor, I'm sorry," I whispered. "I didn't mean to hurt you."

"Stupid William," he snarled. "You can't hurt Igor!"

He stepped forward again.

I knew I couldn't stop him, but I put my hands up anyway. The gesture was enough to make him pause. He stared at me for a moment, then turned away. When he turned back the torchlight reflecting in his eyes showed a pain so deep I knew it had not been caused by my brief gesture.

"You can't hurt Igor. But don't you never, never, never touch Igor on the hump! *Never!*"

He turned away, clumped to the wall, and began

pounding on it. One stone actually began to come loose under the force of his blows. Blood covered his knuckles.

I ran to him, grabbed his arm. "Igor! Listen, Igor, I'm sorry! I won't ever do it again! I promise!"

He kept pounding, shaking me back and forth. For a moment I was afraid I would have my brains dashed out against the dungeon wall. Suddenly he stopped and slumped to the floor. Closing his eyes, he dropped his head against the wall.

"Get bear," he said. "Igor want bear."

I searched frantically for the bear, finally found it in the pile of rags where Igor slept. When I put it into his hands he clutched it without opening his eyes.

I sat down beside him, no longer afraid. For a long time neither of us said anything. Finally I decided I should just go. But when I started to stand Igor opened his eyes. "Why you come see Igor, William?"

Why? Well, I was frustrated because I couldn't get solid answers from anyone. I had hoped that Igor might have some information—though now that I thought about it, that didn't seem likely, especially given the previous night's conversation.

Then I realized the real reason that I had come.

"I like you," I said. "I wanted to talk to you."

"Igor like William," he replied, giving me an affectionate little bop with his bear. He stared at me for a moment, then asked, "Where William come from?"

"I don't know," I replied truthfully.

"Don't know?" he repeated, sounding puzzled.

"No one seems to know," I said, and then I told him the story of how the Baron had found me on the drawbridge.

He looked worried.

"What's wrong, Igor?"

"Don't know," he said, wrinkling his brow so that his deep-set eyes nearly disappeared. "Story make Igor think of something. But what? What?" He began to knock his knuckles against his bald head. "Think, Igor," he muttered. "Think, think. Think, think." Finally he looked up. "Igor hate it when he got to think," he said in despair. He sighed. Then he jumped up and said, "Igor got to go!"

"Go where?" I asked, feeling confused.

"Got to talk to someone."

"Who?"

"Can't say."

"Why not?"

He looked at me for a moment, then picked up his bear and shook it in my face. "See bear?" he asked, as if it were possible for me to miss it.

I nodded.

"Like to get bopped?"

I shook my head, wondering if he was about to bop me for asking too many questions. But I had misunderstood. He was trying to make a point. "Igor don't like to get bopped either. Igor say too much, Igor get bopped."

"You mean someone will hit you with a bear?" I asked, trying to sort this out.

He shook his head. "Bear Igor's! No one else get to bop with it. But like that. Igor don't want to get in trouble. Igor hate being in trouble. Now William go, so Igor can go ask questions."

"Can I go with you?"

"Bad idea!" he said, so fiercely that I decided not to argue.

Annoyed and discouraged, I trudged up the five hundred steps. The last thing I wanted was one more secret, one more thing someone wouldn't talk about. I hated it!

I went to the Great Hall on the main floor. Slipping through the metal bars of the cage that rose from the center of the floor, I climbed onto the back of the huge stone toad that gave the castle its name. This was one of my favorite thinking spots.

I had asked Karl a number of times where the caged toad came from, why it was there, what it stood for. He always told me that he didn't know.

As I thought about it, I realized that whenever he had told me that, I had believed him, had had no sense that he was holding something back from me. It had been different when he talked about the North Tower. Then he had seemed to be hiding something, had almost seemed frightened.

I had one person left to ask: the Baron. Despite the fact that Karl had warned me not to, I decided to try. The problem was, I had been trained early on to wait until the Baron spoke to me before saying anything. So I had never just gone up to him and asked a question before. I decided if I went where he was, he might speak to me. Then I could ask my question.

Despite my curiosity, I felt some reluctance to go to the Baron. Instead of climbing the stairs to the library I found myself meandering about the Great Hall, examining with fresh interest things with which I was already quite familiar—the huge chandelier that hung from the middle of the ceiling, the suits of armor that lined the wall, the collection of cannonballs from great battles that rested on the mantelpiece of the enormous fireplace. When I found myself counting the cannonballs for the third time I decided I had put things off long enough and returned to the stair.

I found the Baron at his desk in the library, absorbed in a book. As I waited for him to notice me I studied his face. It was red and round, as was his nose. His white eyebrows sprouted out in all directions. He had a bushy white mustache, puffy sideburns, and a fringe of hair around his pale, bald head. Each time he turned a page he blew through his lips, making a wet, fluttering sound.

Suddenly he looked up and noticed me. His eyes were enormous, intelligent, and penetrating—the only

truly intimidating things about him, actually, but so ferocious that when he turned them on me I wanted to sink into the floor.

"Hello there, Gerald," he said cheerfully. Then he slammed the book shut and walked away.

I clenched my fists, trying to decide whether I was angrier about losing my chance to ask about the tower or the fact that the Baron couldn't be bothered to remember my name.

I looked for another opportunity to ask about the tower at dinner. But Karl was dining with us, and I didn't want to bring it up in front of him. Candles flickered in the candelabras. Spiders worked furiously in the corners. Karl stared at his plate. Hulda bustled silently back and forth. I tossed pieces of hard bread to the rats that scurried along the walls. The only sound was that of the Baron slurping his soup.

I went to bed frustrated and angry.

A strange thing happened that night. The noises began to change. Before, they had always had a sad, faraway quality. Now they were louder, almost impatient. Again I began to think they were trying to say something.

And then, so distinctly that there could be no mistaking it, they called my name.

## CHAPTER SEVEN
# MUCH ADO ABOUT NOTHING

I pulled the covers over my head and hunkered into my bed. What was going on? Were the voices really speaking, or had I somehow imagined it?

*Was I going crazy?*

I waited for them to speak again—dreading the sound, yet wanting confirmation that I wasn't losing my mind. But they didn't come again. At least not that night.

I huddled under the covers for hours, not falling asleep until the night was nearly gone, and only then because I simply could not stay awake any longer.

When I went to visit Igor the next day he wasn't there. I began to worry. Had something happened to him? I wished desperately that he was in his cell so I could talk to him.

Back upstairs, I tried again to speak to the Baron but couldn't find a chance. Though he was in the library until noon, he was immersed in a book and simply did not notice me. Then a visitor arrived—the second in as many weeks, which was surprising, since we often went months with no one approaching the castle save the old farmer who delivered our supplies. The visitor was tall and wore a dark cloak with a hood that covered his face. The Baron did not seem happy to see him but did not try to send him away, either. They went to a private room to speak. That was the last I saw of the Baron for the day.

I wandered the halls, angry and frightened. Finally I decided to go to the North Tower. Maybe I would see something that would help me understand what was happening.

The door to the North Tower was in an alcove, set slightly aside from the main hall. As I stared at it, I was terrified to see it begin to change. Its solid wooden face had always been bare of decoration. But as I watched, a design began to appear. Slowly at first, and then faster, silvery lines began to form, creating a five-pointed star woven all around with strange signs and symbols.

Then, from the other side of the door, something called my name.

I turned and ran.

That night, which was Halloween, the voices returned, louder than ever. Shortly before midnight they began to whisper my name again: "William. Willllliaammmm."

"Go away," I said, pulling the covers up to my neck and wishing that Igor was with me.

"Williammmm! Come open the door!"

"Stop bothering me!"

"Willliammmmm, Williammmmm . . ." On and on, until I thought I was going to lose my mind.

I was terrified, but the voices were impossible to ignore. And after a while their call began to draw me, pull me. It was hard to resist them. I was tired. I had barely slept for the last several nights. And I admit I was curious.

"Willllliaaammmmm! Willllliaaammmm, come open the doooor!"

I flung the covers aside and got out of bed. I told myself that I was going to shut the voices up, going because I was angry.

I don't know if that was true. I do know that when

I heard the clock strike midnight a change came over me. Though the voices were calling more insistently than ever, I suddenly felt that this was a truly bad idea. But when I decided to turn back, I *couldn't*. Whatever was going on had me in its grip, and I could no more turn back than I could stop breathing.

I was wearing nothing but my nightshirt. The stone floor was cold against my bare feet. But those feet continued walking as if they were not mine at all, carrying me toward the North Tower.

"Williammmm," moaned the voices. "Come open the door! We're so eager to be free."

I tried to stop, tried to grind my feet against the floor so that they wouldn't move. I couldn't do it.

Soon, too soon, I was standing in front of the door.

The silvery design that had appeared to me earlier in the day was back, glowing a warning through the darkness. "Danger!" it seemed to say. "Keep away. *Do not open!*"

The door said one thing, the voices another. "Open the door," they pleaded. "Oh, pleeeaaase, William, open the door!"

I found myself reaching forward and pulled back.

The voices grew more demanding. "William—the door!" they whispered fiercely. "William—the door!"

Again I felt my hand reaching forward.

"No!" I cried. Squeezing my eyes shut, I forced my hand back to my side.

"Williammmmmm!" moaned the voices, so sadly it was as if the castle itself was speaking with a broken heart. "Don't leave us here. Open the door. This is the time. This is the hour. This is why you are here! William, open the door!"

*This is why you are here!* The words burned inside me like the torch in Igor's cell. Why was I here, why had I been brought to the castle? Was it to open this door? Was that my purpose, my job? I had felt so long as if I didn't really belong, didn't fit, that the idea that this was my reason, that this was what I was here to do, was more than I could resist. I trembled as I felt my hand begin to rise.

"William," crooned the voices, "we will love you forever if you just open the door for us. Open the door. . . ."

Tears in my eyes, I reached forward.

"William!" cried a new voice from behind me. "Don't!"

I didn't turn to see who was speaking, didn't need to; I knew the voice well. Besides, I couldn't have turned if I had wanted to. I was rooted to the spot.

"William!" cried Karl again. "Wait!"

"The door, William!" hissed the voices, more urgently than ever. "Now, before it's too late. Open the door before the time is gone. This is why you are here. This is why we will love you. The door, William. *Open the door!*"

Reaching forward, I put my hand on the latch.

"William, don't do it!" cried Karl.

Too late. When my hand closed on the latch the door that had been locked for all those years burst open so violently it nearly knocked me over. I had not pulled on the door; it was as if my touch itself had been enough to free whatever was behind it.

A shriek of triumph filled the night as *something* came rushing past me—something real, yet no easier to touch than mist. It was shapes and voices, a sense of strange power flowing past and around me. The air rang with mad shrieks, and a kind of gibbering laughter went careening down the hall.

I slid to the floor, shivering with fear and remorse.

After a few minutes Karl crawled over to sit beside me. I saw that he was trembling, too. "I wish you hadn't done that," he said.

"What *did* I do?"

"I'm not sure." He leaned his head back against

the wall and closed his eyes. "I've been trying for years to figure out what was locked in there, William. Whatever it was, I think it would have been better for you to leave it there."

A strange silence had settled over the castle. The door to the tower hung open. The area beyond it was dark, darker even than the dungeons, as if a curtain of darkness was suspended across the doorway. You couldn't even see the steps. A draught—bone-chilling, heart-chilling—flowed from the opening. I stood to close the door.

"Wait," said Karl. "I want to look up there."

I was surprised; he was braver than I thought.

Stepping past me, he peered through the door. After a moment he stepped back. "Can't see a thing," he muttered, shaking his head.

"Hold the door open," I said. "I'll go up a few steps."

He looked at me in surprise. But I had spent so much time wandering around in the darkness that this didn't seem as bad to me as it obviously did to him. I did want him to hold the door, though. I feared that if it swung shut, it might not open again for hundreds of years.

I stepped over the threshold and cried out in shock. What waited on the other side of the door was *nothing.* For a moment I thought I was falling, because there was nothing beneath my feet. Then I realized I wasn't moving at all, simply floating. The darkness was so complete I felt as if I had been swallowed by night itself.

Reaching forward, I tried to find something to touch.

Nothing.

I tried to walk. Nothing to press my feet against.

*"Karl?"*

"I'm here. Where are *you?*"

"Here! Just through the doorway!"

"I can't see you. Come back!"

His voice came from behind me, which made sense. Turning my head, I saw the door frame. Just past it stood Karl. Though he was staring straight at me, it was obvious that he could not see me. At least he wasn't far away. I tried to turn so I could go back through the door. But with nothing to push against, I couldn't move.

"Karl! I don't think I can get out!"

"What do you mean?"

"I don't know how to explain. There's nothing here. *Nothing!* But I can see you; you're only a few feet behind me."

"Should I come in for you?" he asked, sounding as if it was the last thing in the world he wanted to do.

"No! If you do, we might both be stuck. See if you can find a rope. Maybe you can pull me out."

"I'll be back as soon as I can."

"Wait!" I started to say. "Don't leave me. . . ."

Too late; he was gone.

I looked around nervously. Nothing. Nothing in all directions, nothing above, nothing below, nothing to the right or the left. Only the door behind me, floating in the darkness.

I glanced up. How far above me did this space extend? To the roof of the tower? Beyond?

How far down?

Wondering what kind of emptiness stretched beneath me made my stomach queasy, and I tried to push the thought away. I began to concentrate on trying to get out instead. Though I didn't seem to be able to move forward or backward, I found that by squirming I could twist my body around.

After several minutes of this I was facing the door.

As I floated in the nothingness, hoping Karl would come back soon, my mind began to play tricks on me. The door looked as though it was starting to close.

Suddenly I realized it was no trick of my mind; the

door *was* closing! The movement was slow, so slow I could barely notice it. But if I looked away, counted to a hundred, then looked back, it was clear the door's position had changed.

It could have been caused by anything—a draft in the hall, gravity, magic. I didn't care what was doing it, I just wanted it to stop! After a moment I wanted it bad enough to try to make it stop by talking to it.

"Don't shut, door," I pleaded. "Don't leave me here in the darkness."

From beyond the door something laughed.

## CHAPTER EIGHT

# THE MORNING AFTER

My spine tingling with terror, I stared at the slowly moving door. "Who's there?" I cried.

No answer.

"Why are you doing this?"

No answer, save a slight creak from the door.

*"Stop!"* I screamed.

It didn't work; the door continued to move.

What would happen when it closed completely? Would I be trapped in this nothingness forever? I squirmed and writhed, trying to push myself closer to the door. It was hopeless, like one of those dreams where you run and run but can't seem to move. I strained my muscles trying to throw myself toward the opening.

The door, slow as it was, moved more than I did. Inch by inch it was shutting me in. Soon the light, the world, Igor, and everything would be gone. I would be lost to the nothingness.

Less than two inches to go.

"Please stop!" I begged.

Again that unearthly chuckle. And then another sound: feet running down the hall. At first I thought it was Karl. Then I realized I was hearing many feet, as if there were dozens of people out there. The thought was startling. That would be more people than I had seen in my entire life.

"Help!" I cried. "Please help me! Open the door!"

Pattering, pounding, slapping, the bare feet came on. A sudden uproar of voices, then the door was wrenched open.

"Hurray for William!" cried several voices.

"Nilbog, Nilbog!" cried several others.

"Who are you?" I shouted.

But my rescuers, whoever they were, were gone. I could hear the feet running in the opposite direction.

And one more sound—a wail of dismay, made by the same voice that had been laughing at me before. Then, for a long time, silence. I continued to twist and turn, trying to work myself closer to the doorway.

Footsteps again.

"Who's there?" I cried nervously.

"It's me—Karl." A moment later I saw his handsome face at the door. His hair was tousled, and he looked frightened. "Are you still there?" he called, looking straight at me.

"Yes! Do you have the rope?"

"Yes. It wasn't easy. Here."

The rope came snaking through the doorway, three or four feet to the right of me.

I stretched, but it was useless.

"I can't reach it," I called.

Karl pulled the rope back and tried again. It took four attempts before he got it close enough for me to grab it. Then it was only a matter of seconds for him to pull me back into the hallway. I came flying out of the darkness with a *pop!* and fell in a heap at his feet.

"Thank you!" I gasped. "I thought I was never going to get out of there!"

"I had begun to wonder myself," replied Karl.

Now that I was closer, I could see that he looked even more disheveled than I had realized.

"What's going on out here?" I asked.

"I don't know, but it's plenty strange. I think we should take shelter. It doesn't seem safe in the halls."

Even as he said that a crash sounded from the floor below us.

"What was that?" I asked.

"Who knows? Let's get behind a door while we can."

"As long as it's not that one!" I said.

Karl nodded and swung the door shut. We decided to go to my room, since it was the closest. Once inside, we barred the door, then braced it shut with a chair for good measure.

Outside the noises continued as footsteps raced up and down the stairs, doors slammed, unknown objects crashed. Twice something rattled at my door, trying to open it. The bar held firm. The first time, whatever was on the other side of the door screamed in rage. The second time it laughed. The voices seemed to be different.

I felt safer having Karl with me. After a while, in spite of the uproar, exhaustion overwhelmed me, and I slept.

When the morning sun woke me I saw Karl sprawled in a big chair near the fireplace, snoring softly. Mervyn crouched on the windowsill, staring at him curiously. His whiskers were twitching as if to say, "What's *he* doing here?"

I closed my eyes and listened carefully.

All was silent. Was the chaos over? Or had it simply ended with the morning light, to be resumed when darkness fell?

"Karl?" I whispered.

"Mmmmmm?"

"Karl, let's go see what happened."

"Mmmmmm," he said, rolling his head to the side.

*"Karl!"*

He sat up quickly, almost falling off the chair. "What is it? Did something get in?"

"No, I think it's over. At least for now. Let's go out and look."

He rubbed his hands over his face, then nodded warily. "I guess we'd better."

I took off my nightshirt and got into some clothes. Moving cautiously, we went to the door. Karl moved the chair, and I lifted the bar. Then we stopped. I could tell that neither one of us wanted to open the door. Finally I reached forward and eased it slowly open, half expecting something to wrench it out of my hands and come bounding into the room.

The hall was empty.

As I put out my head, the clock on the first floor began to strike.

I counted, wondering what time it was.

Two bongs.

"That doesn't make any sense," I said. "It can't be past noon."

Karl looked troubled. "You're right. But that clock has never been wrong in all the years I've lived here."

Side by side we stepped into the hall. I peered about warily, waiting for something to jump out at us.

After a moment I noticed something odd.

"Karl, does the hall seem strange to you?"

"In what way?"

"Well—it's *clean*."

He blinked in surprise. "You're right!"

We walked along, staring up at the ceiling, down at the baseboard. The familiar cobwebs were gone. The dust in which I had written my name the year before, which had been there until last night, was gone as well.

"What's going on here?" I asked.

Karl shook his head. "I don't know."

We passed an open door. I knew the room—I had often entered it from the secret passage. It was a bedroom much like mine. Only it was spotlessly clean.

That was strange enough. What made things even stranger was the fact that the furniture was all upside down.

61

We were stepping into the room to take a closer look when we heard a scream from below.

"That's Hulda!" shouted Karl.

I followed him into the hall. He reached the stairs before me; he was halfway down when his feet flew into the air. "Yow!" he cried, crashing onto the stairs and sliding to the bottom.

"Are you all right?" I called. I was still on the stairs, worried that if I continued down them whatever had happened to Karl would happen to me as well.

He moaned, then said, "I don't think there's anything broken."

"What happened?"

"I slipped on something." He turned to look up at me. "Be careful coming down."

Moving cautiously, I clutched the rail and bent to examine the steps. Four steps below me—about where Karl had lost his balance—I noticed something shiny. I ran my finger over it. It felt familiar. I lifted my finger to my nose and sniffed.

"Soap!" I shouted.

"What?"

"The step was coated with soap. That's why you slipped."

Karl frowned. "What *is* going on around here?"

"We can figure it out later. Right now we need to see what's happening to Hulda."

As if to emphasize my point, we heard another scream from below. This time I realized the emotion behind the scream wasn't fear, it was anger.

"Maybe we should take our time after all," I said.

Karl nodded. "Probably safer that way—for more than one reason."

Moving cautiously, checking for booby traps, we continued toward the main floor of the castle. One floor above the main floor we had to climb through a maze of twine that had been woven in the hallway. It was like trying to work your way through some gigantic cobweb.

When we finally reached the main floor we followed the sound of Hulda's voice to the laundry rooms. She was shouting now, not screaming, and I got the impression the Baron was with her.

"Look at this," she bellowed when she saw us at the door. "Just look at it!"

She was holding up a sheet. It was freshly laundered and in fact looked cleaner than any sheet I had seen in years.

It was also completely tied in knots.

So was every other piece of cloth in the room. Shirts, sheets, trousers—everything that had accumulated in the months since Hulda had last tackled the washing—had been carefully washed and then tied into knots. The Baron sat in a corner, pulling at one of the knots with his teeth.

"Let's have some breakfast," he said, putting down the sheet. He stood and began to lead the way to the kitchen. The door was partially open. When he pushed it all the way a bucket of water fell onto his head.

That wasn't the end of the mischief. The sugar bowl was glued to the table. When we finally got it loose it turned out to be full of salt, a fact I discovered by spooning it into my coffee, which I ended up spitting across the table.

"Well, what was it?" I finally cried. "What was behind that door?"

"I don't know," said the Baron, though it was clear that he knew which door I was talking about. "I've been trying to find out for years. I know my grandfather locked something away up there over a century ago, but I have never been able to find out what it was. I do think it might have been better if the door had been left shut."

He stared at me with those astonishing eyes of his. I felt like crawling under the table.

"What do we do now?" asked Karl.

The Baron shook his head. "I don't know. Prepare for the night, I guess. We'll need to find ways to bar the doors to our rooms more securely."

The two of them began to discuss how we could protect ourselves that night. When it became clear they were not going to ask my opinion, I decided to leave the table. I wanted to see what else had happened overnight. I also wanted to get away from the others because I was feeling enormously guilty for having opened the door, and I didn't know how to make up for it.

I went to the main hall. More mischief. Someone had tied a ribbon around the neck of the great stone toad. The bars of its cage had been bent, as if it were being invited to escape. The helmets from the suits of armor had all been switched around so that none of them matched. I was starting to put them back in place when a voice whispered, *"William!"*

To my astonishment, I saw Igor beside one of the suits of armor. He was standing as close to the wall as his hump would allow, as if he were trying to blend into the stones.

"Igor remembered!" he said, shaking his bear triumphantly.

"Remembered what?"

He rolled his eyes. "What was in North Tower."

## CHAPTER NINE
# IGOR EXPLAINS

"Tell me!" I said eagerly.

"Come with Igor," he replied.

He led me to a secret passage I had never seen before and soon we were on our way to the dungeons. As we entered one of the long passages that wound beneath the castle I heard a scratching sound behind us, and then the sound of feet running: *pad pad pad, pad pad pad*. All of a sudden a small shape went dashing past us.

"There go one!" cried Igor. He lunged out to catch it, but missed.

"What was *that*?" I asked nervously.

"Wait till we get to Igor's room. Igor explain everything."

As we traveled I heard laughter and scratching, shrieks and moans.

I was glad Igor was with me.

When we finally reached Igor's cell he motioned to his pile of rags with his bear. "Sit, William. Igor got to tell you story."

I sat. He was silent for a moment, and his eyes rolled around in his head as if he were sorting out his thoughts. Finally he began.

"Long time ago, long before William come to live with Baron, Igor used to live upstairs sometimes. We had different Baron here back then, and Igor was his best helper. Igor loved that stupid old Baron, 'cause he would always talk to Igor. He say things like, 'Good Igor,' and 'Stupid Igor,' and 'Out of my way, you fool!' and 'What would I do without you, Igor?' and he only kick Igor once in a while. So Igor love that old Baron.

"Old Baron was good to people around here, and he try to help them. Back then there was goblins running all over at night causing trouble. They lived deep down in the mountains, way in the dark, 'cause they hated the light."

It was the most I had heard Igor say at one time, and the effort seemed to be taking a toll on him. But he pressed on.

"We had all kind of goblins: big ones and little ones, ones with tails and ones with no tails, some with arms so long they got to walk on their knuckles, and some that just roll around. They all had big fiery eyes and sharp gnashing teeth. They used to do rotten stuff. At night they come out of their mountain and go to town. Then they tear things up and scare animals and throw stuff in wells. And if any person come out at night, which mostly no one stupid enough to do, goblins take that person to Goblin Land and make them stay there for ever and ever.

"This make people unhappy and miserable, so old Baron decide to do something about it. He get big book from library and look and look for right spells. Then he turn all them goblins into spirits and lock them in tower and seal door so they can't get out unless someone open it."

I began to blush. But I didn't tell Igor what I had done. I was too ashamed.

"That what 'Most dangerous night' message was about. Night was coming when goblins be most strong, have chance to get out. Now they out!" He looked troubled. "Whoever done that very stupid. Anyway, new Baron don't know how to lock up them goblins. And now that they out they will be getting their bodies back."

Bending low, Igor looked me in the eye and whispered. "That what in these dungeons, William. When Baron made all them goblins be spirits he say to me, 'Igor you brute' (that's what he like to call me: Igor-you-brute), 'Igor,' he say, 'you take them bodies down to dungeons and lock 'em up.' And I say to Baron, 'Why don't we burn 'em?'

"Old Baron whack me on side of head and say, ''Cause we need their bodies to hold 'em here. Burn bodies, spirits get loose and cause more trouble!'

"So Igor carry all them goblin bodies down to dungeons. It scare Igor plenty, 'cause they not really dead. They keep twitching and moaning and groaning, 'cause they want their spirits back so they can go make more trouble. Baron say, 'Igor, stay here and watch them bodies. If they start moving too much, like they coming back to life, you come get me.'"

Igor looked down at his hairy hands, which hung helplessly in his lap. "That long time ago. After while Igor forget about them goblin spirits locked up in top of castle. He just keep watching bodies. That Igor's job. After another while old Baron gone. No one come to talk to Igor. No one know about Igor. But Igor keep doing job.

"Now someone let them spirits out, and they come

69

back to get their bodies. There gonna be trouble, William—more trouble than Igor can think about."

We sat for a long time, staring at the wall.

Finally I said, "What can we do, Igor?"

He looked at me with fear in his eyes.

"Only one thing to do. Got to go see Granny Pinchbottom."

*"What?"*

Igor looked at me with concern. "William got bad ears?"

"My ears are fine. What did you just say?"

He looked confused, then repeated, "William got bad ears?"

"No, before that—about Granny Pinchbottom."

I could see him racking his brains. Finally a light came on in his eyes. "William and Igor got to go see Granny Pinchbottom!" he cried triumphantly, proud at having dredged the words up from his memory.

"But Karl told me Granny Pinchbottom didn't exist."

Igor gave me a bop with his bear.

"I've heard scary things about her," I whispered.

"Probably all true," said Igor, squeezing his bear to his chest so tightly that it almost disappeared into his beard. "She scare Igor, that for sure."

"Then why are we going to go get her?"

"'Cause goblins scare Igor worse. 'Cause Igor done bad thing by not watching goblins good enough, and now Igor got to fix it."

By that logic, I was in on this, too. Of course, it meant that I would have to do what I had never done in my life: leave the castle and go outside. I was fascinated—and frightened again.

"Time to go," said Igor. Stepping out of the cell, he took the torch from the bracket in the wall. "Goodbye, home," he said, as if he never expected to see the place again. Taking a firm grip on his bear's hind leg, he started down the hall. "Watch out for goblins," he whispered, in a voice I was sure could be heard ten feet away. "They all over down here now."

I nodded and began to scan the hall for any sign of the creatures. We had been traveling for only a few minutes when I heard footsteps behind us. I looked back.

The footsteps stopped; I could see nothing.

"Igor!" I hissed.

He walked on, making no sign that he had heard me.

I scurried to catch up with him.

The footsteps began again. This time I tugged at the back of Igor's coat, being careful not to get near his hump. He spun around, ready to do battle, and seemed surprised when he saw no one but me.

"I think we're being followed," I whispered.

Igor peered into the darkness behind us. After a moment he handed me the torch. "Igor walk in back now!" he said.

I nodded and lifted the torch above my head. Its flickering flame made shadows dance around us. My imagination insisted on turning them into goblins waiting to attack. The echo of our footsteps seemed to take on a threatening sound.

"Go that way," said Igor after a moment.

"Which way?"

"That way!" he said. I looked behind and saw that he was pointing to the left.

The tunnel was dank, and water trickled down the walls. I stepped into a puddle. It was cold. A rat scurried along the wall beside me; it was big, much bigger than Mervyn.

The corridor curved to the right. We stepped through an arch. I screamed as something jumped onto my back.

## CHAPTER TEN

# INTO THE WORLD

"Get it off!" I cried as the thing wrapped its long fingers in my hair. "Igor, get it off me!"

I heard Igor grunt. I swung around, trying to dislodge the attacker myself, and saw at least eight more of the creatures coming at us.

I didn't have time to study them. I remember only a sense of exaggerated features: big eyes, huge noses, flapping ears. Beyond that it was chaos as they came bounding out of the darkness.

The goblin on my back was shrieking with delight. Igor was roaring with fury. "Get off that William!" he cried, lashing out with his bear and whacking the goblin that clung to me. It bounced away, taking some of my skin with it.

The others hurried on, screaming, shouting, grabbing at Igor. He lashed out with his bear, swinging it to the right and the left. "Bop!" he cried. "Bop, bop, bop! Take that, goblin! And that, and that!"

I found that by using the torch I could drive some of them back. Igor's frenzied strength was terrible to see. In only a moment the goblins fled shrieking into the darkness.

I collapsed against the wall. "Thank goodness *that's* over!"

Igor shook his head. "Maybe over—maybe not. Come on, we got to keep moving. Bear done good," he added, patting the bear on the head and giving it a little kiss. "Igor love bear."

We moved more cautiously now, fearing another attack at any moment. After a time we came to a stone bridge that crossed a gap in the floor. I wondered if the stream below was the same one I had found the night I met Ishmael.

A similar set of steps led down to the edge of the stream. "Don't put foot in water," said Igor. "Might not get it back."

Remembering how I had dipped my hands in the

water that other night, I shivered and squeezed against the wall.

We followed the stream through a stone tunnel. At the point where the stream disappeared we came to a crude door. Igor pushed it opened. The tunnel on the other side cut through soil rather than stone and was braced with rough-cut timbers. The earthen walls were moist and slippery. The little crooked things sticking out from the walls frightened me, until I realized they were roots.

After several minutes we reached a stone wall that blocked any more progress.

"Hold bear," growled Igor.

I took the bear. Igor began to grunt and groan. Soon the stone wall was replaced by a dazzling circle of light.

I followed Igor through the hole.

I was outside!

"Blah!" said Igor. "Don't like daytime. Hurt eyes."

I knew what he meant. The sun was so bright compared to our flickering torch that at first I found it hard to see out there. Blinking, I looked back at the comfortable darkness we had just left and gasped in astonishment when I saw the enormous boulder Igor had pushed aside. He was even stronger than I had realized, almost stronger than I could imagine.

We had crossed under the moat and come up not far from its shore. On the other side of the murky water loomed Toad-in-a-Cage Castle. I had never seen it from the outside before, and I was amazed at its size. The four tall towers formed a sort of box around the castle itself, which squatted beneath them—almost like a toad in a cage. Suddenly I realized that the mist that had always surrounded the North Tower was gone.

I shivered and looked away.

The air was sweet and clean, but the sky was so high and far off that I felt small and unprotected. Though it was exciting to be outside, I missed the safety of four walls and a roof.

"Come on," said Igor, tapping me lightly with his bear. "We got to go."

We followed a path that led up a tree-covered hill. A light breeze rustled through the dead leaves that swirled around our feet. I liked their spicy smell, which I had never experienced before. Sunlight fell in patches around us, dappling through the brightly colored, half-bare trees. The path was faint, but Igor seemed to know it well. He led me up hills and down, across land I had studied from the library window yet never set foot on. After an hour or so we crested a hill that overlooked the village. "Are we going to go there?" I asked eagerly.

Igor shook his head. "Igor don't go to town during day."

I sighed. It would have been exciting to go where there were other people—though as I stared longingly at the town I began to realize that it wasn't what I had expected, that it was drab and bare, the streets nearly deserted.

"Where is everyone?"

Igor shrugged. "Not many people anymore. Town used to be bigger, brighter." He paused, then added, "Used to be more fun."

"What happened to it?"

"Who know? Not Igor. Come on—we got to keep going."

We took a wide path around the village.

Troubled as I was by what had happened, I was also half giddy with the excitement of being outside, overwhelmed by the sights and smells and sounds of the world that I had never entered before. Igor had to bop me three times to get me to settle down. "Quiet, William!" he urged. "Got to be quiet!"

Toward the middle of the day he took me into a shallow cave, where we sat to rest while the sun passed its high point. "Too bright," muttered Igor, scuttling to the back of the cave. "Igor don't like too bright."

Late in the afternoon we started out again. Along the way Igor showed me various plants that we could eat—sometimes fruits, sometimes leaves or stems, sometimes even roots.

As it grew dark we entered the forest.

Leaves rustled beneath our feet. The branches over our heads cut scars across the pale white moon, which floated huge and full above us.

I had seen the forest before, had spent hours studying it from my window. But being inside it was different. From the inside it felt wild and strange, more frightening and beautiful than I could have imagined. Thick trees, gnarled and weather-worn, loomed in the moonlight like sentinels challenging our right to be there.

The trail we followed led along the edge of a great gorge, a deep and rocky drop filled with mystery and moonshadow. I tried to stay as far from it as I could, but something about it seemed to grip me. Over and over I found myself peering into those wild, rocky depths.

So I was the first one to see the goblins.

"Igor!" I cried. "Watch out!"

It was too late. A band of them swarmed over the edge. Ignoring me, they threw themselves toward Igor, leaping and clawing.

Roaring with anger, Igor lashed around him with the bear. "Bop! Bop! Bop!" he cried. Goblins flew in all directions. But there were more of them now than in the first attack, many more.

"Leave him alone!" I cried, flinging myself into the fray, trying to pull the goblins away from him. But for each one I managed to dislodge it seemed that two more took its place. They swarmed over Igor like ants over a sweet.

The fourth goblin I pulled from Igor turned on me with eyes of fire and an open mouth that seemed to take up half its face. With a cry of rage it flung me aside.

I crashed into a tree, and the world went black.

When I opened my eyes again the battle was over. Igor, still thrashing wildly, had been bound and was being carried toward the gorge on the backs of a dozen goblins. Even as I staggered to my feet, they disappeared over the edge, chanting. "Nilbog, Nilbog, Nilbog!"

"Igor," I cried, as if that would bring him back. "Igor!"

Something hit me from behind. I staggered forward and fell facedown in the leaves.

• • •

This time when I opened my eyes the moon was low in the sky. The night was silent.

I was alone.

My head hurt. I put my hand on the back of it and felt a sticky lump.

Crawling to the edge of the gorge, I tried to stare into its depths. They were lost in shadow. The only thing I could make out was much closer at hand. On a ledge about five feet below lay Igor's bear.

## CHAPTER ELEVEN

# THE REWARD

A wave of despair washed over me. Dropping my head into my arms, I began to sob.

My crying was interrupted by a hand on my shoulder. I rolled over, ready to fight, and found myself staring at a beautiful woman. The thought that she might be my mother flashed through my mind, then disappeared. My mother had abandoned me, for whatever reason, eleven years before. I wasn't going to find her here in the woods.

"Who are you?" I asked, trying to keep my voice from trembling.

She didn't answer right away, only smiled. The last of the moonlight seemed to catch in her enormous eyes, to rest gently on her long, dark hair. Her smile brought slight wrinkles to the sides of her mouth and eyes.

"Who are you?" I asked again.

"I have many names," she said, reaching out a hand to help me up. "Around here I am mostly known as Granny Pinchbottom."

I was so surprised I let go of her hand and fell backwards. "You're supposed to be old and ugly!"

She turned away from me. When she turned back her beauty had vanished. Her hair hung limp and gray around her shoulders, and her nose curved out and down so that it pointed at her warty chin.

"What you want is what you will see," she cackled.

I drew back in shock.

"Be careful!"

Looking behind me, I saw that I had come within inches of falling over the edge of the gorge. I took a step forward.

"How did you change like that?"

"None of your business! Follow me."

Turning, she walked into the forest, not looking to see if I was actually following her.

"Wait!" I cried. "I have to get something."

She didn't wait. Though I was worried about losing

sight of her, I couldn't leave Igor's bear behind. Hoping I would still be able to see Granny Pinchbottom after I retrieved it, I scrambled over the edge of the gorge and grabbed the bear.

When I came back up the old woman was gone.

"Wait!" I cried again, running forward. "Wait for me!"

Within minutes I was totally lost, not only unable to find Granny Pinchbottom, but also unable to find my way back to the gorge. Clutching Igor's bear, I glanced around nervously, wondering if more goblins lurked in the woods.

A twig snapped behind me.

I spun, ready to lash out with the bear, and found myself face-to-face with a girl. She had big eyes, and dark hair that hung past her shoulders. She wore a ragged brown shift, cinched at the center with a leather belt. A leather pouch hung at her right side, a long knife at her left.

"What are you doing here?" I cried in surprise.

"I live here. What are you doing here?"

I could think of several answers. I settled for the most immediate one: "Looking for Granny Pinchbottom."

The girl's eyes widened. "You're a brave one!"

"I suppose so," I replied. It was beginning to sink

in that this was the first girl I had ever seen. She was interesting-looking. "What's your name?"

"Fauna. And yours?"

"I'm called William. Do you know where I can find Granny Pinchbottom?"

"Are you sure you want to do that?"

"I have to. Something bad happened, and I think she can help. At least my friend thought she could help. But something happened to him, too, so now I have to try to find her on my own." I paused, then added, "Actually, she found me a few minutes ago, but then she disappeared again."

"Disappeared? That doesn't sound like her."

I sighed. "She told me to follow her. I asked her to wait, because I had to get something, but she didn't. By the time I had gotten what I needed, she was gone."

Fauna laughed, a sound even prettier than the stream that ran through Igor's dungeon. "Granny Pinchbottom doesn't wait for anyone. Come on—I'll show you where she lives. But I won't go inside with you. You'll have to do that on your own."

The way she said this did little to add to my confidence.

"Where do *you* live?" I asked as we began to walk.

"In the woods, not far from here. And you?"

"I live in Toad-in-a-Cage Castle."

She looked more surprised than ever. "What are you doing out here?"

"I don't want to talk about it."

"Suit yourself," she said, quickening her pace so that I had to hurry to keep up with her. She knew the forest well, finding easy paths through brambly hedges that I would have thought impassable, picking her way across streams where the stepping stones were invisible to my eye until I saw where she placed her feet.

The next-to-the-last stream we crossed was about fifty yards down from a waterfall nearly as tall as the towers of Toad-in-a-Cage Castle.

About forty-five minutes after passing the waterfall we came to a small clearing. In the center of the clearing stood a cottage with rough walls and a thatched roof. The light shining from its windows flashed in changing colors.

"That's it," whispered my guide. "Granny Pinchbottom's place. Good luck!"

She stepped away and disappeared among the moonshadows.

"Fauna!" I whispered urgently. "Wait!"

No answer.

I stared at the cottage nervously. Taking a deep

breath, I walked forward and knocked on the door.

"Come in!"

The creaky voice was familiar; it went with the second face Granny Pinchbottom had shown me.

I pushed open the door. The single room of the cottage was illumined by three large logs that burned in the stone fireplace. A large cauldron hung over the fire, steaming and bubbling.

In a rocking chair near the fire sat Granny Pinchbottom. A huge black cat lay sprawled across her lap. It gave me an arrogant stare, then jumped down and stalked across the room, as if disgusted by my very existence.

"You took long enough getting here," said the old woman.

"You didn't wait for me," I replied with more bravery than I felt.

She shrugged. "Why don't you tell me what happened?"

To my astonishment, I did just that. Despite the guilt and embarrassment I felt over having let the goblins loose, I opened my mouth and poured out the entire tale.

As I spoke Granny Pinchbottom reached into the bag next to her. My eyes widened as I watched her pull out a strand of light and begin weaving it through her fingers as if she were making a cat's cradle.

As I finished my story she tied the light into a knot, then reached into the bag and drew out a silver amulet. It dangled from a silver chain. Popping open the amulet, she tucked the knot of light inside.

"Take this," she said, handing it to me.

"Why?" I asked in surprise.

"Call it a reward."

"For what?"

She threw back her head and cackled. "For releasing the goblins. I appreciate it very much."

## CHAPTER TWELVE

# THE GOLDEN COLLAR

I stared at her in horror. "You *wanted* me to let them out?"

She stopped laughing and leaned toward me, her hooked chin pointing toward my face. "I have been working for the release of those goblins for more years than you can imagine," she hissed.

*"Why?"*

Her answer astonished me. "Because we need them out here. This land is dead and lifeless without them."

"I don't understand."

"You have no way of knowing what things were like before the goblins disappeared, William, so you can't know what we've lost. But things were different then.

The world around here was more joyous, the people happier, the land more bountiful. When the goblins were locked away, when their wild energy was imprisoned, much of that went with them."

I was so intent on what she was saying that it wasn't until sometime later that I realized she had called me by my name, even though I had never mentioned it to her.

"But if they were good for things, why were they locked away?"

"Come closer."

I was only a few feet away as it was. When I hesitated Granny Pinchbottom didn't say anything, just stared at me.

After a moment I stepped forward.

She still didn't say anything.

I knelt down. Now my face was just slightly below hers. Reaching out, she took my cheeks between her hands and stared straight into my eyes.

"That which is joyous, that which is lively, that which is free of fear is often most feared. The goblins had their kingdom underground, but most of them lived out here, among the people. When a goblin attached itself to a house it would care for it. Though it would often work minor mischief, it always did more good than harm—which is more than many humans can say. If the goblins occasionally led a child to play in the mud—and they did—they more often saved that child from genuine danger."

"What about the people they stole away to Goblin Land?"

The old woman snorted. "Some people *chose* to go to Goblin Land—which is properly called Nilbog, by the way. Other people, who couldn't understand such a choice, decided it wasn't a choice at all and spread rumors that their neighbors had been stolen. Fear began to grow. People began to resent the goblins."

She made a spitting noise, a sound of disgust. "The Baron at the time, who was the grandfather of the Baron you know, had a blind heart. He didn't understand play, didn't believe in mischief, didn't know how to laugh. The goblins' pranks annoyed him beyond endurance, and he never realized that they were the ones who kept his castle spotless, the ones who polished his wood and shined his windows and tended his gardens with secret tricks that made them grow in a way his own gardener never could. After a great deal of study, and with the help of a powerful wizard, he managed to lock them away."

She shook her head, and her eyes looked pained. "A great gloom fell over the land. At first no one realized what had happened, for much of the good the goblins did was done in secret—usually at night, which was the time they liked best. But somehow the houses were never as neat, the gardens never as productive, the children never as safe as they had been. This was once a land of plenty. Now the village limps along, growing smaller every year, because fewer children are born. That's why I have been working toward the goblins' release. But there was one thing I didn't count on, one thing I hadn't anticipated."

The tone in her voice made my stomach tighten. "What was that?"

She grimaced. "Their *rage*. I should have expected it: When you imprison something, you change it. And the goblins have been changed."

"Are they evil now?"

Granny Pinchbottom shook her head. "I don't think they're evil. But they're so angry you wouldn't be able to tell the difference. Trouble is coming—big trouble. Unless . . ."

She trailed off and stared at me. I could feel her examining me, assessing me.

"Unless what?" I asked, unable to keep the words

inside, though I had a feeling that silence might have been smarter.

"The goblins follow the example of their King. It's more than that; they are *connected* to him in a way that can only be called magical. The problem is that the King has gone quite mad as a result of what happened, lost his head altogether. I think if he can be cured, the others will follow."

"How can that be done?"

"I have three things to give you," she replied, which wasn't quite an answer but seemed to be leading in that direction. "The first was the amulet, which will provide you with light in the darkest places. Here is the second."

Reaching into the bag next to her, she withdrew a piece of cloth. When she shook it out I could see that it was a cloak. "Put it on," she whispered.

I took it from her hands and stood. The cloak fit my shoulders as if it had been made for me. A golden clasp shaped like an oak leaf held it fast about my neck.

"Raise the hood."

I did as she directed. To my astonishment, I disappeared!

"Hey!" I cried. "What happened?"

"The cloak is working," she chuckled, rubbing her bony hands together.

"But I can't see myself!"

"Of course not. You're wearing a cloak of invisibility."

"This is wonderful," I said, thinking of all the ways in which I could use such a thing.

"It's yours—if you agree to take on my mission."

I knew there had to be a catch. "What's the mission?"

Again she reached into the bag. This time she drew forth a band of gold about the length of my arm and an inch wide. It had a buckle on one end and three green stones in the center. Looking directly into my eyes, she whispered, "I want you to fasten this around the neck of the Goblin King."

Fingers trembling, I reached for the golden collar. "Why don't you do it yourself?" I asked. "You know more about this kind of thing than I do."

She smiled, showing a few yellowed teeth. "I'm just an old woman," she said, sounding pitiful.

"But not always . . ."

She shrugged. "The truth is, I'm too powerful. The goblins would know I was coming before I got anywhere near the King. They have ways of sensing people like me."

I sighed. "What do I have to do?"

"First you should rest. Then have something to eat. After that I'll give you a map to Nilbog, and you can be on your way."

That sounded good—I was terribly tired. But I couldn't rest if Igor was in danger. When I said something about that Granny Pinchbottom replied, "I don't believe the goblins will hurt him. At least not yet. Far more likely they will imprison him. Possibly mock him. As for you—you'll be little help to anyone if you don't get some rest."

Suddenly I felt a great weariness creeping over me. Was Granny Pinchbottom casting a spell on me? Considering how little sleep—and how much trouble—I had had in the last few days, it didn't take magic to explain my exhaustion. The mere mention of sleep might have been enough to remind my body and brain how tired they were.

"That way," she whispered, pointing to a cot near the fireplace.

I stumbled in the direction she pointed. Clutching Igor's bear, I fell onto the cot and slept like the dead.

When I woke I found myself lying facedown in a pile of leaves. I sat up, confused and frightened. What had happened? Where was Granny Pinchbottom?

I looked around. As near as I could tell, I was in the clearing Fauna had led me to the night before. The only thing missing was the cottage.

Beside me lay Igor's bear and the drawstring bag from which Granny Pinchbottom had taken the amulet, cloak, and collar.

"Granny Pinchbottom?" I called. "Are you here?"

No answer, save the wind moving through the leaves.

Suddenly the clearing grew dark. Looking up, I saw thick clouds massing in the west. From the look of them, a big storm was coming.

I opened the bag and peeked inside. The three items Granny Pinchbottom had given me were there, as well as some paper packets that turned out to contain food—bread, cheese, and even a sweet.

Well, she was as good as her word; she had said that after I slept she would feed me.

She had also promised a map, which I found at the bottom of the bag. It was drawn in green ink on yellowed paper. The clearing where I now stood was marked in the lower left-hand corner. (I knew it was the clearing where I stood because it was labeled "You are here.")

According to the arrows, I had to walk back the way

Fauna had brought me the night before. At the next-to-the-last stream we had passed I was to turn and head for the waterfall.

Thunder rumbled overhead. I glanced up. It wouldn't be long before the whole *sky* was a waterfall. Folding the map, I tucked it into my shirt, picked up the bear and the bag, and started to walk.

As I stepped from the clearing something ran out of the bushes and grabbed me by the leg.

"Gotcha!" it cried in a squeaky voice. "Gotcha, got-cha, gotcha!"

I screamed and shook my leg, trying to dislodge my attacker. It was no use; the little thing was fastened to me tighter than a fresh scab. I jumped around in terror for a minute, then realized two things. One, I wasn't going to get it off of me. Two, it didn't seem to be hurting me. It was holding on, but not biting or scratching. My heart still pounding, I stopped yelling and looked down.

The creature clinging to my leg was about a foot and a half tall. It had big yellow eyes and a big nose. A tail stuck out of its ragged little britches, which were held up by a single suspender hooked over its left shoulder. Its large, pointed ears flapped when I shook my leg.

"Gotcha!" it cried, looking up at me.

"What are you?"

"Herky!"

"You're a herky?"

"No, no, no! Herky my name. Am goblin, I am! Fierce and bad, bad and fierce!"

"Why are you holding on to me?"

"Herky gotcha!"

"Yes, you've got me. But why do you want me?"

"Herky bad!" it cried, as if that answered everything.

Cautiously I reached my hands toward the creature, ready to draw them back if it made any sign of trying to bite me. It didn't. Grasping it around the middle, I pulled it away from my leg, then lifted it to the level of my face.

"How bad are you?" I asked.

"Very bad, very most bad," it cried in a high-pitched voice. "Herky fierce bad goblin. Fierce sad—*bad*!"

Aha! "Why are you sad?" I asked, ignoring his attempt to correct himself.

"Herky lost," he sighed. "Other goblins all gone back to Nilbog. Herky can't find it. Herky mad! Herky sad! Herky bad, bad, bad!"

"Herky hungry?"

The little goblin clacked its teeth together, which I took to mean yes. Setting him down, I took out one of the packets Granny Pinchbottom had left me and handed him some bread.

"Yum!" he said eagerly, opening his mouth to take a huge bite. No sooner had he closed his mouth on the loaf than a look of dismay widened his yellow eyes and he spit the wad of bread to the ground. "Ptooie!" he cried. "Bad food. Food bad!"

"What kind of food do you like?" I asked, feeling rather annoyed at the loss of some good bread.

Herky scrambled up my leg and peered into the bag. "Got lizards?"

"No, I don't have any lizards! And get your face out of there," I added, grabbing him by the back of the neck and pulling him away from the bag. I didn't know if he could tell what I had in the bag just by looking at it, but I didn't particularly want to have a goblin learn I was carrying a cloak of invisibility.

"Yow!" cried Herky as I pulled him away from the bag. "Yow, yow, yow! Boy mean! Mean boy!"

"Goblin rude," I replied, setting him on the ground. I was about to squat so I could talk to him face-to-face when it occurred to me that doing so would make it very easy for him to bite me on the nose. I stared at him for a moment. Was he an enemy or not?

"Gotcha!" cried Herky, grabbing something from the leaves and popping it into his mouth.

I squatted, but not too close. "My name is—"

Before I could finish Herky looked past my shoulder. "Yow!" he shouted. Then he disappeared into the bushes.

## CHAPTER THIRTEEN
# "THIS WAY TO NILBOG"

"What was *that*?" asked a familiar voice.

"Fauna!" I cried, turning around. "What did you do that for?"

"Do what for?" she asked, sounding hurt, and a little angry.

"Scare him away!"

"I didn't do anything to scare anyone. I walked up, and that thing shouted and ran off. What was it? And don't forget to apologize for yelling at me for nothing."

I didn't want to apologize. But Fauna was right; she hadn't done anything wrong. "Sorry," I muttered.

"Have you got something caught in your throat?"

100

"I'm *sorry!*" I shouted, wondering if all girls were this difficult to deal with.

"You're forgiven. Now what was that thing?"

"A goblin," I replied, enjoying the look of shock the word created on her face.

"The goblins are gone," she said. "They've been gone for over a hundred years!"

"Well, they're back now."

"How could that be?" she asked, her hand dropping to the knife she wore at her side.

Despite what Granny Pinchbottom had told me, *how* the goblins had returned wasn't something I particularly wanted to discuss. Actually, I didn't want to discuss anything. I just wanted to get rid of Fauna so I could get on with my mission.

"It doesn't matter how it happened. What matters is what happens next. If you'll excuse me, I've got a job to do."

"I'll help."

"How can you say that? You don't even know what I'm going to do."

"It has to do with the goblins, doesn't it?"

"Well, yes."

"Then I'll help. I don't want them around here again."

I started to say that I didn't want help. But that wasn't true. I needed all the help I could get. I just didn't like having it shoved down my throat.

"Look, I don't think you understand about the goblins," I said. "They're not as bad as you think—at least, they didn't used to be. There's no telling what they're like now."

"What are you talking about?"

My answer was lost in a sizzle of lightning that was followed by a roll of thunder so loud it made both of us jump.

"I don't have time to stand here and talk," I said. "I have to go to Nilbog."

Her look of surprise reminded me of the morning Hulda had accidentally swallowed a fly. "You're going to Nilbog?" she whispered. "What *for?*"

"My friend has been stolen by the goblins."

"I thought you said they weren't so bad."

"I was just telling you what Granny Pinchbottom told me!" I said in exasperation. "Listen, I have to get moving. It's going to rain soon, and I don't want to be standing here when it happens." (Though I thought it would be fun to stand in the rain sometime; I had never done it before.)

"Well, let's go," she said, taking a deep breath

and pushing her hair back over her shoulders.

"Didn't you hear me? I'm going to Nilbog!"

"Didn't you hear me? I'm coming with you."

"Don't you have to go home or something? Won't your parents be upset?"

Her laugh was like falling water. "I don't have any parents. I live alone."

I thought about trying to outrun her. I didn't think I could manage it while trying to read a map.

Another roll of thunder shook the darkening sky.

"Let's go," I said. "We can discuss this while we walk."

She nodded, and I started off. After a moment I said, "Since we're going back the way you brought me last night, it might be faster if you lead the way."

She nodded again and took the lead. For the first few minutes we walked without talking. I waited for her to start asking questions again. She didn't. I was just opening my mouth to speak when I heard a rustling in the branches above me. Something dropped from the tree and landed on my head.

"Gotcha!" it cried, grabbing me by the hair and bracing one foot against my right ear. "Gotcha, gotcha, gotcha!"

"Herky!" I shouted. "Don't do that!"

"Boy mad?" he asked, sounding genuinely astonished.

"Yes, I'm mad," I said, reaching up to pluck the little creature from my head. "Ouch! Let go of my hair!"

"Yellow hair nice," said Herky, as I pried his long fingers out of my scalp. "Herky ba-ack!" he cried when I had lowered him so that he was in front of my face again. "Don't let funny person hurt him!"

"What funny person?" I started to ask. Then I realized he was talking about Fauna.

"You'd better behave, goblin, or I'll do more than hurt you," she said fiercely.

"Fauna, leave him alone. He may be able to help us."

"Hunh! I don't think much of goblin help. What's he going to do when we get to Nilbog?"

"Hooray for Nilbog!" cried Herky, squirming out of my grasp and dropping to the ground. "Nilbog good!"

I wanted to tell Fauna what Granny Pinchbottom had told me about the goblins, but I wasn't sure how much of it I should say in front of Herky. I wasn't sure *what* to do about Herky, though it did seem safer to have him with us than have him following us. "Do you want to come with us?" I asked.

"Yep, yep, yep! Herky go with butterhead boy and nighthair girl. Don't make Herky mad! Herky fierce!"

He clacked his teeth to demonstrate his ferocity, and I began to question the wisdom of my decision. Small though he was, those teeth could do a lot of damage.

"Brilliant," said Fauna, ignoring Herky and looking at me.

"Oh, be quiet," I said irritably. "Let's get going."

I loved walking through the woods, despite the dark sky, the rumble of thunder, the threat of pouring rain. I loved the sound of rushing water that was almost always with us, sometimes in the distance, sometimes close at hand, and the softness of the leaf-covered ground, and most of all the mysterious oldness of it all.

Herky kept running off to examine things, scrambling up trees to chase squirrels, even disappearing into small holes in the ground. But he always came loping back sooner or later, panting and snarling and announcing, "Herky bad! Bad Herky! Better be afraid, butterhead boy!"

"My name is William!" I snapped after the third time he called me this. I regretted my words immediately, remembering that Hulda had told me names were magical, and much could be done by someone who knew your true name. I had thought it was pretty silly at the time, but with everything that had gone on during the last few days, this didn't seem like a time to take chances with things like that.

"Yucko!" cried Herky when we came to the first stream we had to cross. "Herky don't like water!" Then he scrambled up my leg and insisted on riding on my shoulder.

"All right," I said. "As long as you don't pull my hair!"

"Bad Herky like butterhead hair," he said, grabbing a handful and giving it a tug just light enough that I couldn't really call it a pull.

I sighed and crossed the stream. Shortly after we got to the other side Herky spotted a bird and threw himself into the air in a vain attempt to catch it.

"Bad bird!" he muttered when he fell face first among the leaves. "Herky mad at bird."

It took another half hour to reach the waterfall. We had gone about half the distance when I heard a pattering above us. It sounded like thousands of tiny feet. At first I didn't know what could be making the sound. Then I realized that it was . . .

"Rain!" cried Herky. "Yike, yike, yike! No rain! Make it stop, William!"

"I can't stop the rain, Herky."

"Put me in bag! Herky hate rain."

He was shivering, and his funny little face looked

so miserable I actually wanted to help him. "All right, just a minute," I said. "I have to clean it out first."

Going behind a large tree, I removed the cloak, the amulet, and the golden collar. The amulet I placed around my neck. I rolled the cloak, which was made of a light fabric, and tucked it inside my shirt. I stared at the golden collar for a moment, wondering what to do with it. Finally I pulled up my shirt and tried wrapping it around my waist. To my surprise, it fit. Was it bigger than I thought, or had it stretched somehow? How big was the Goblin King's neck? I fastened the collar over the cloak, holding it in place.

The rain was falling faster.

"Hurry!" pleaded Herky from the other side of the tree.

"Make sure he stays where he is!" I called to Fauna.

"Look, goblin," she muttered, "you make one move toward that tree, and I'll have a goblin skin hanging on my wall."

"Girl bad!" cried Herky. "Help, William, help!"

I stepped back from around the tree. "You didn't have to terrorize the poor thing," I said.

Fauna shrugged and thrust her knife back into its sheath.

"Do you have room for these?" I asked, holding out

the food packets Granny Pinchbottom had given me.

She took them and tucked them into the pouch she carried at her side. When I opened the top of my own bag Herky jumped in as if it were his long-lost home.

"No rain!" he cried, pulling the edges together. "Bad rain go away!"

I secured the top and swung the bag over my shoulder.

Fauna took the lead again. At first the trees sheltered us from the rain. But as the drops began to fall faster and the top levels of the forest grew soaked, the rain began dripping through. Cold and uncomfortable, I began to wish that someone was carrying *me* in a pack on his back.

We began to run, leaping over stones and roots that were growing slick with moisture. Thunder and lightning played overhead, and Herky shouted "Yow!" every time the sky rumbled with their power.

The waterfall was even taller than I remembered. We heard it before we saw it, and as we started toward it I was amazed at how loud it became. Our path followed the stream that flowed from the base of the falls. The trees did not offer much cover here, and the rain began to pound against us.

"What now?" asked Fauna as we drew near the falls.

"Let's go under there," I replied, pointing to a rocky overhang where we could get out of the rain.

The waterfall itself poured over a sheer cliff that blocked any other progress in that direction, landing in a wide pool that foamed with the force of the water striking it.

We ducked into the space I had indicated. It was not deep enough to be a cave, but did have sufficient room for me to study the map without exposing it to the rain.

I extracted the map from my shirt. To my surprise, it was bone dry. I was even more surprised when I unfolded it.

"What's the matter?" asked Fauna, when she saw the look on my face.

"This has changed since the last time I looked at it!"

"Who gave it to you?"

"Granny Pinchbottom."

She shrugged, as if that explained everything.

I looked at the map again. The bottom left corner still said "You are here." But instead of the clearing it showed the waterfall where we were now standing. According to the diagram above it, we were supposed to go *under* the waterfall.

"Herky's not going to like this," I muttered, showing the map to Fauna.

"Who cares? Let's get moving."

We stepped back out into the rain—which was nothing compared to the deluge that engulfed us when we climbed the rocks leading to the waterfall. The spray alone was enough to soak us. When we reached the base of the falls itself we found no secret, dry path hidden beside it. We had to go straight through.

Nodding to each other, we stepped forward.

"*Yow!*" cried Herky as the water hit us. "William bad!"

The pounding water nearly tore the bag from my hands. It was almost impossible to keep my footing, and I slipped three or four times. I couldn't see, couldn't hear anything other than the roar of the falling water.

Then suddenly we were through and on the other side. Even though I was soaked to the skin, it was a relief to be out of the falling water.

Herky didn't seem to think so. "Bad, bad, bad!" he sputtered. "Bad William! William bad!"

"Oh, be quiet!" I snapped. Swinging the bag in front of me, I opened the top and pulled him out by the scruff of his neck. He squirmed out of my hand and shook himself vigorously.

We were in a large cave. Though I had expected this side of the waterfall to be dark, the space was suffused with a soft glow. After a while I realized that it came from some kind of fungus that was growing all over the rocks.

"Look!" said Fauna.

I turned in the direction she was pointing. Resting on a boulder was a large wooden sign that said, in neat letters, THIS WAY TO NILBOG.

On the bottom someone had scrawled *Turn back now, while you still can!*

## CHAPTER FOURTEEN

# THROUGH CAVERNS DEEP AND DARK

The caves seemed to go on forever. Sometimes there were signs to point the way, sometimes not. We passed through chambers slick with moisture, chambers dry as toast, chambers where some strange source of heat made us feel as if we were walking through an oven. Some places were so high and vast I felt as if we were outside again—except there was no sky, only a distant darkness.

I thought of Igor often. What were the goblins doing to him? I hoped we would find him soon—though what we would do when that happened, how we might rescue him, I had no idea. At least I had Granny Pinchbottom's gifts to help me.

The first of those gifts became useful sooner than I expected. This was because the glowing fungus began to disappear as we traveled away from the waterfall. Though Herky seemed to have no trouble traveling in the darkness, Fauna and I found it harder and harder to go on.

I took out the amulet. It cast no light. I shook it, wondering if there was some secret to making it work. Nothing. But when the last of the fungus was gone, and the darkness had become complete, the amulet began to glow all by itself—faintly at first, then brighter and brighter, until I had to take it away from my neck. I held it over my head like a lantern, and it provided more than enough light for us to continue.

We stopped to eat in a small chamber that had walls streaked with veins of red and umber. Stalactites and stalagmites filled it like fangs run amok, growing everywhere instead of in an orderly half circle. Leaning against one of the stalagmites, I asked Fauna to pass around the food packets I had given her when I had made room in my bag for Herky.

"No lizards?" asked the little goblin wistfully when the food came his way.

When I shook my head he ran away. He came back

a little while later, smiling. I didn't ask him what he had done.

"What are we going to do when we get to Nilbog?" asked Fauna, cutting a slice of cheese with her knife.

"I don't know if I should say," I whispered, gesturing toward Herky. He sat a couple of feet away, licking his toes with his long orange tongue.

Fauna nodded. I was glad to drop the conversation. Other than the fact that I was going to try to put the golden collar around the Goblin King's neck, I had no idea *what* we were going to do when we got there.

Herky was not so uncertain. "Party!" he cried.

"What?" asked Fauna.

"Herky be glad glad glad to be home. Home good. Herky say have party!"

"Listen, Herky. The goblins will be glad to see you. At least, I assume they will," I added, wondering if they might consider him as much of a nuisance as I sometimes did. "But I don't think they'll be glad to see Fauna and me."

He looked troubled. "You goblin friends," he said at last. "Herky friends, goblin friends!"

"Even so, it might be better if you didn't tell anyone about us," I said. "We could be a secret."

"Herky bad at secrets," he replied, tugging on one of his huge ears.

"Maybe I should skin him now and get it over with," whispered Fauna.

I glared at her. She glared back.

When I was done eating I took out the map and examined it by the light of the amulet. According to the bottom corner—the section marked "You are here"—we were in a chamber that had three possible exits. We were supposed to leave by the one farthest to the right.

I returned the food packets to my bag. "Let's get going," I said.

Fauna pushed herself to her feet. Herky scrambled up my leg. "Want ride!" he said.

We threaded our way among the stalagmites and stalactites, coming at last to the far wall. Though the map said we should take the passage farthest to the right, the passage in the center had a wooden sign in front of it that said, as had others along the way, "This way to Nilbog."

"Now what do we do?" I said in exasperation.

"What's the matter?" asked Fauna.

I explained.

"Follow sign!" said Herky. "Goblin sign good! Good goblin sign, be home soon!"

"I wouldn't follow a goblin sign for anything," said Fauna. "It's either crazy, a lie, or a trap."

"This way!" said Herky. "Herky remember now! This way to home!"

"Have you been this way before?" I asked.

"Yes, yes, yes! This way good!"

"Are you going to trust him, or Granny Pinchbottom's map?" asked Fauna.

"Me, me, me!" cried Herky. "Herky want to go home!" Scrambling off my shoulder, he shot into the middle tunnel.

"Herky!" I cried. "Come back!"

"Leave him. We're better off without him. For all you know, he was a spy anyway."

Before I could reply, Herky's voice came echoing out of the tunnel. "Ouch! Ouch, ouch, ouchers! William! Help Herky, William!"

Right tunnel or wrong, I couldn't leave him if he was in trouble. "Come on," I said. Without waiting to see if Fauna would follow me, I raced into the tunnel. It didn't occur to me that she didn't have much choice, that I had the only source of light. If she didn't follow me, she would be left alone in the darkness.

She did point this out to me afterward.

I didn't have to go far to find out what was wrong.

The tunnel, between three and four feet wide, was strewn with large stones of all shapes and sizes. Herky had been scrambling over one of them and had managed to get his tail caught in a crack. As I came up to him he was howling and trying to tug it loose.

"Ow, yow, wowie ouchers!" he shouted. He yanked at it, which only pulled it more tightly into the crack of the boulder.

"Herky, stop! You'll never get it out that way."

"Owie ouchers!" he cried, continuing to tug at it.

"Stop!" I yelled, grabbing him around the waist.

At that moment Fauna joined us. "I could cut it out for you," she said, reaching for her knife.

"Yow!" cried Herky. He tried to scramble up to my shoulder, but of course his tail held him in place. His sharp fingers dug into my arms.

"Stop!" I said. "Fauna isn't going to cut off your tail—are you, Fauna?"

"I ought to, considering the trouble he's causing," she replied. But she took her hand off the knife.

"Just help me," I said.

I held the amulet over the rock, and we examined the situation. Herky's frantic efforts to free himself had wedged his tail deeply into the cleft in the stone. Even worse, the abuse had made it start to swell.

"This isn't going to be easy," said Fauna.

I nodded. "You'll have to hold still, Herky, or you're going to make it worse."

"Owie!"

"Fauna, I'll hold him—you try to get the tail loose."

Setting the amulet on a nearby rock, I locked my hands around Herky's waist. Fauna began to work at releasing the tail. Despite her harsh words her fingers were gentle as she tried to pry it free. "This is going to hurt," she whispered after a moment.

"No owies!" cried Herky.

"Look, you have three choices," said Fauna harshly. "You can stay here forever. I can cut off your tail. Or you can suffer quietly while I loosen this thing, which wouldn't be stuck at all if you had stayed with us to begin with."

"Girl mean," whimpered Herky, snuggling against me.

Fauna ignored him and continued to work at the tail. After a moment she took out her knife.

"*No!*" cried Herky.

"Be quiet. I'm not going to cut it off, I'm going to pry it loose. William, hold him so he doesn't wiggle."

I tightened my grip around Herky's waist. With the cutting edge pointing down, Fauna slipped her knife

118

under his tail. She began to rock the blade up and down, trying to lift the tail with the wide, flat edge of the blade.

"Owie, owie, owie," whispered Herky, burying his head against my shirt and squirming back and forth.

Fauna didn't tell him to be quiet. She just kept rocking the knife. Herky clutched my shirt more tightly.

"Got it!" said Fauna a moment later.

"It's all right, Herky," I said. "Fauna got it out."

"Herky hurty!"

I wasn't surprised. His tail was swollen and bruised. The skin where it had been caught was torn, and something green was oozing out. I wondered if it was goblin blood.

"We should wrap that," said Fauna.

Turning Herky in my lap, I pulled one side of my shirt out of my britches. "Cut a strip off the bottom of this."

Fauna used her knife to start a tear, then ripped a strip of cloth about fifteen inches long from the bottom of the shirt. When she was done I tucked the shirt back in so it would hold the cloak and the collar in place. Fauna wrapped the strip of cloth around Herky's tail and tied it.

As we were getting up to go I heard a rumbling

119

sound. It came from where we had entered the tunnel.

"What's that?" I whispered.

"Rocks," said Fauna. "Or maybe one big rock."

Then I heard something even worse than the sound of moving rocks. It was the sound of goblins laughing.

"Come on!" I shouted. Snatching the amulet, I raced toward the opening.

It was too late. It had been sealed.

"Uh-oh," said Herky. "Maybe this way bad after all."

I took out the map. It was blank, except for the bottom left corner. Where it used to say, "You are here" it now read, "DANGER! YOU HAVE LEFT THE PATH! RETURN AS SOON AS POSSIBLE!"

## CHAPTER FIFTEEN

# OVER THE RIVER AND THROUGH THE ROCKS

A half hour of clawing at rocks, a half hour of breaking our nails and bloodying our fingers convinced us there was no possibility of returning the way we had come.

"This is your fault," said Fauna to Herky. "We should have left you here to rot."

"Girl mean," said Herky. But he said it without much spirit.

Since we couldn't go back, we decided to go forward—though I had some concern about whether we might be walking into a goblin trap.

Holding the amulet aloft, I led the way past Herky's rock on through the tunnel, which was narrow but very high.

After a while the wall on our right disappeared, leaving a high wall to our left and flat, open space to the right. I wondered if the way out lay somewhere in that direction. But if we went that way, we could quickly become lost in the emptiness. By sticking with the wall we could always retrace our steps—though what good that would do us I didn't know.

Sometimes I thought I heard footsteps behind us. But when I stopped to listen more carefully the footsteps—if that's what they were—stopped, too.

None of us spoke much, not even Herky.

The rock wall to our left was smooth. Sometimes water trickled down its surface. When we got thirsty enough we would lap some of the water from the wall. It was cold and sweet.

The decision to stay with the wall proved wise, because after a while the floor to the right disappeared as well. Now we were walking along a ledge about a foot and a half wide, with a rocky wall to the left and a sheer drop to the right. I held the amulet out over the dark drop. Its light did not reach to the bottom.

When we came to a notch in the wall big enough for the three of us to sit safely back from the edge of the abyss we stopped for a rest. I passed around some food.

"Icky!" said Herky. But he ate some of the bread; there was nothing else for him.

I was worried that we might run out soon, but when I closed the packets they seemed as full as they had the very first time I opened them. I smiled. Though the map had lost its usefulness after we foolishly left the path, at least *this* bit of Granny Pinchbottom's magic was still working.

We decided to sleep. I gave my brain a strict command that I was not to roll over. It wasn't that far to a drop that seemed to have no end.

I don't know how long I had been sleeping when Herky's voice woke me. When I opened my eyes to scold him I saw that he was asleep himself. He was jerking and twitching and muttering "Cold and dark, dark and cold! Nothing, nothing, nothing!"

After a moment I realized he must be dreaming about the North Tower. Remembering the horror of the place, I laid my hand on his forehead. This seemed to settle him, and soon he was sleeping peacefully again.

I did not go back to sleep myself. I still had my eyes open when Fauna whispered, "William?"

"What?"

"I'm afraid."

"Me too."

"What are we going to do?"

"Keep going."

"That's what I thought."

A while later we did just that.

Before long the wall to the left disappeared as well. Now we had about a foot and a half of path—and that was it. On our right and our left was a sheer drop to a depth we could not guess.

By the light of the amulet I could see the path curving through the void ahead of us, winding left, right, rising, dipping, disappearing into the darkness.

Far beneath us I could hear the sound of a rushing river.

The path grew narrower—a foot wide, then less. Every step became a matter of life and death. I felt like I was walking along the edge of a giant razor. And still I thought I could hear footsteps behind us.

We began to grow tired again, but there was no place to rest. More than once I stumbled in my exhaustion.

The path stopped at a sheer wall. For a terrifying moment I thought we were blocked, that after all this we would have to turn around and go back. But when I lifted the amulet a little higher I could see an opening about eight feet to our right. There was even a way to get over to it—if you consider a ridge of stone as wide as your hand a way to get somewhere.

We didn't have much choice. Slipping the silver chain over my head, I flipped it around so that the amulet hung against my back. Then I pressed my belly against the wall and began inching toward the opening.

Herky came close behind me. His long, nimble fingers and toes seemed to make this fairly simple for him.

Fauna came last, her face set and grim.

I felt better when I put my hand around the edge of the opening—and better still when I pulled myself inside and saw that it went on for a way. Taking the amulet off my neck, I thrust it back out so Fauna could have light to finish the trip.

Once she was inside we began walking again. It wasn't long before the tunnel began to grow narrower, more enclosed. Looking up, I could see the rock ceiling above us, something I had barely seen in all the time we had been in the caverns. Soon the ceiling grew lower. The walls grew closer together.

"I don't like this," said Fauna.

I didn't like it either. "Herky," I said, "run ahead. Come back and tell me how small the tunnel gets."

"You bet, William!" Scurrying between my legs, he disappeared into the darkness. A few moments later he came dashing back, scrambled up my legs, and put his hands around my middle. Then he jumped down and ran off again. When he returned the next time he climbed all the way to my shoulders and put his hands next to my head.

"What are you doing?" I asked.

"Measuring!" he replied as he jumped down and disappeared into the darkness. After a bit his voice came back down the tunnel. "I think you fit, William!"

I didn't particularly like the sound of that. I turned to Fauna. She shrugged. I knew what she meant: What else was there to do?

I started forward. Before long I had to drop to my hands and knees. The stone was smooth and cold beneath my fingers. Soon the ceiling was so low that I began to scrape my head. I stuffed Igor's bear into the bag Granny Pinchbottom had given me, then tied the bag to my foot. Dropping to my belly, I began to crawl.

The sides of the tunnel grew so close together that they began to scrape against me. I felt as if I were being squeezed by a giant hand. Hoping Herky was right when he said that I would fit, I stretched my hands ahead of me, and pulled myself forward.

"Hiya!" said Herky, sticking his face into mine. Then he thrust out his longer fingers and messed up my hair.

"Herky!" I yelled, "don't do that!"

"William mad?" he asked, sounding hurt.

"Just nervous. How much further do I have to go?"

"Herky go check," he said, turning and moving easily through the tiny space that was giving me such trouble.

He didn't come back.

"Herky?" I called.

No answer.

*"Herky?"*

No answer.

"He's probably playing some kind of game," said Fauna from behind me.

I pulled myself forward, hoping she was right.

The tunnel grew even tighter. I couldn't move to the right or the left, couldn't raise my head more than an inch or two without running into the rock. Against my will I began to picture the vastness of what lay above me, the mountain of rock held up by—what?

My out-of-control imagination saw it slipping, crushing me deep in the earth where no one would ever find me.

"Stop!" I commanded myself out loud.

"Why?" asked Fauna.

"Sorry. I was talking to myself." Staring ahead, I shouted, "Herky!"

No answer.

I pulled myself forward, wondering how accurate his measurements had been, and whether I might soon find myself hopelessly jammed into this ever-diminishing tunnel. Tighter it grew, and tighter still, until I felt as though I were breathing stone.

I began to think little things were crawling over me. The fact that nothing seemed to live down here didn't stop my frenzied imagination from inventing "rock-worms"—nasty creatures that burrowed through stone and human flesh. I began to imagine them working their way into my skin.

Forward, slowly forward, ever more cramped. Would the tunnel become so tight it would scrape away the cloak and collar I had tucked inside my shirt? I slid back a few inches and picked up the silver chain in my teeth, to keep the amulet from being squashed between my chest and the stone floor.

"Are you all right?" whispered Fauna from behind me.

"Yes," I replied, though that was only half true.

"Does it get any better?" she asked nervously.

I spit out the amulet chain. "Not as far as I can tell."

She didn't reply. Lifting the amulet with my teeth again, I crawled forward. Soon the tunnel was so tight that I couldn't bring my arms back to my sides. They were extended full length in front of me, and that was where they had to stay.

My nose began to itch.

Inching forward, inching forward, I came to a place where the space between the roof and the floor of the tunnel was so narrow I wasn't sure my head would fit through. When Herky had checked the size of my head he had used nothing but his hands. How accurate could his measurement have been? If I went forward, would I jam my head into a place from which I could never release it?

"Herky!"

No answer. Where had he gone?

And then, behind us, the sound of goblins laughing.

Fauna grabbed my foot. "Did you hear?" she hissed.

"I heard!" I replied. Turning my head sideways, I squirmed forward. Cold rock pressed against my temples. Pulling with my fingertips, pressing with my feet, I moved another inch, then stopped. I could go no further. Let the goblins laugh. They couldn't get at me here anyhow.

"William!" said Fauna. *"Keep going!"*

"I can't!"

But that wasn't true. When I moved my head to the left I found a spare half inch. Emptying my lungs to make myself flatter, I pushed forward again.

Something cold and scaly grabbed my hands and began to pull.

## CHAPTER SIXTEEN

# NILBOG

In a matter of seconds, and despite my screams of terror, I had been pulled from the tunnel. My face was bleeding, my ribs felt as if Hulda had been kneading them like bread dough, and my heart was pounding so hard I thought it was trying to beat its way out of my body.

Looking around did nothing to calm me; I faced a ring of goblins, in a variety of shapes, sizes, and colors. Their clothes were ragged, their long feet bare. They had large eyes and even bigger ears. Some had knobby heads and bulbous noses, others huge mouths filled with pointy teeth. All were grinning at me unpleasantly.

I did not see this by amulet light. The silver chain had caught on a rock as I was dragged from the tunnel, and the amulet had been ripped from my body. The light now came from odd torches carried by three of the goblins. Each torch consisted of a stick with a basket at one end. The baskets were packed with the glowing fungus we had seen when we first entered the caverns, though this variety seemed even more luminous.

As if losing the amulet wasn't bad enough, once the goblins had me out of the tunnel one of them lifted me into the air while another detached Granny Pinchbottom's bag from my foot.

"Give that back!" I shouted.

The goblins just laughed.

I was glad I had put the cloak and the collar inside my shirt before we entered the caverns. But the fact that the goblins now had Igor's bear nearly broke my heart.

"William?" called Fauna from the tunnel. "William, what—?"

"Fauna, go back!"

My warning was too late. A goblin with particularly long arms had reached into the tunnel and grabbed Fauna's hands. A few moments later he had dragged her out. Though she looked as battered and bruised as

I felt, she launched into a stream of angry cursing. Her language did little more than make the goblins snort. One took her knife and dropped it into the pouch he wore at his side.

"Herky!" I shouted. "Where are you?"

The little goblin crept out from behind one of the others. "Herky bad!" he whispered miserably.

"I told you not to trust him," said Fauna.

"What shall we do with them?" asked the biggest of the goblins, who had a nose the color and shape of a sweet potato.

"Take them to the King!" cried another.

"The King!" cried the others. "Take them to the King!"

I was swept from the ground and thrown over the shoulder of one of the goblins. Another goblin did the same with Fauna. Then they set off, singing:

> A present for the King,
> A present for the King,
> There is nothing better than
> A present for the King!
>
> It's something young and sweet
> And maybe good to eat!

There is nothing better than
A present for the King!

They sang without stopping until I didn't know what
would be worse: being eaten by the King or having to
hear the stupid song one more time. My only consola-
tion was that at least we were going in the right direction.

As we traveled I was astonished by the goblins'
wild energy. Not only did they sing, they climbed,
jumped, ran, wiggled, and bounced all over the place.
It seemed there was always one or another of them
scrambling up a stalagmite, swinging from a stalactite,
crawling up a wall, leaping overhead, or in one way
or another being somewhere besides the floor of the
cave. At some points there were more goblins in the
air than on the ground.

I might have found this all hilarious if I had not
been trapped on the shoulder of a goblin who was
acting just like all the others—which meant that every
now and then I found the floor suddenly about ten
feet further away than it had been, or realized that the
goblin carrying me had just leapt over some bottom-
less-looking pit that I would never in a million years
have considered crossing without a bridge.

When the goblins started playing leapfrog across a

narrow stone bridge that stretched over a pit of molten lava I just closed my eyes and prayed for the journey to end.

After what seemed like hours a cheer went up among the goblins. I opened my eyes. We were on the edge of a cliff.

Below us lay Nilbog.

"All right, boy, now you walk!" said the goblin who had been carrying me. He swung me to the ground. Before I could recover from my ride he yanked my hands behind my back and bound them with a rough cord. Fauna's goblin did the same, which started her cursing again.

As we picked our way along the narrow path that led down the cliff I had time to study our destination.

Nilbog was far bigger than I had expected. Housed in a vast cavern, it was lit throughout by the same glowing fungus the goblins used for their torches. The fungus grew alongside the paths that meandered through the city, wound around the poles that had been erected wherever two paths crossed, filled window boxes, and even covered entire roofs. Several large areas were oddly dark, as if something had happened to the fungus, but overall there was so much of it that the whole city was suffused with a dim greenish glow, as if dawn was always coming but never arriving.

It was a city of stone and water. On the far side of the city a wide river rushed over a tall cliff, creating a huge underground waterfall. This river flowed through the center of the city, where it was crossed by numerous oddly constructed bridges, most of them covered by the glowing fungus. Water collected in pools and reservoirs, then poured out in streams that sometimes disappeared into the tops of buildings and then flowed out the bottoms.

Rivers and streams flowed in from other directions, too. All of them ran toward the center of the city, which was its lowest point, to gather in a large lake. In the center of the lake, rising from a stony island, stood a castle. Seven towers sprouted at odd angles from its sides. Rickety bridges stretched from tower to tower, and even from where we stood I could see goblins scrambling along them.

As we entered the city I was astonished to see huge jewels—emeralds, rubies, sapphires, and diamonds—used as decorations on the bridges. The streets and paths wound this way and that, seemingly without plan or destination. After a while I realized that the place was almost totally free of straight lines and corners. The buildings were all helter-skelter, higher on one side than on the other, rounded at the edges. Oddly enough, it looked kind of cozy.

What made the city frightening were the thousands of goblins running madly about the streets, swinging from the lampposts, leaping from roof to roof, and screaming at the darkness. I thought to myself, *It's as if everyone has gone crazy.* Then I remembered what Granny Pinchbottom had told me.

I remembered the few moments I had spent in the tower where the goblins had been imprisoned. The goblins had been there for over a hundred years!

I shivered.

Goblins screamed about "wicked humans" as we passed them in the streets. More than once things were thrown at us. But the goblins who had captured us also seemed intent on protecting us, and they shouted at the others to leave us alone, because we were "presents for the King!"

A long stone bridge stretched from the shore of the underground lake to the castle. Pillars carved in strange shapes lined the edges of the bridge. Huge jewels studded its surface.

We entered the castle through tall wooden doors that opened into a long hall leading to the Throne Room.

We had nearly reached our goal. But how was I going to put the collar on the King?

The Throne Room was vast and filled with goblins. They were hooting, screeching, hanging from the ceiling. In a couple of places circles had formed around pairs of goblins who were pulling each other's noses in what seemed to be some form of ritual combat.

Great urns of glowing fungus—some sitting on the floor, some mounted on tall columns—provided the weird green light by which we saw all this.

At the end of the room, on a dais four steps high, stood a stone throne.

On the throne sat a wooden box.

Goblins began to scream and jeer as our captors hustled us along the huge hall. Soon we were standing in front of the throne. An old goblin wearing a golden chain around his neck sat on the third step of the dais. Was he the King? If so, why was there a box on the throne?

"What do you want?" asked the old goblin.

"We have a present for the King!" said our leader.

The old goblin nodded. With a groan he got to his feet and climbed to the throne. I expected him to move the box and sit down. Instead he rapped sharply on the top of the box.

"Who is it?" asked a gravelly voice.

"It's Borg, Your Majesty," said the old goblin. "There is someone here to see you."

"All right," grumbled the voice. "Open the door."

The old goblin moved his hand to a latch and swung open the entire front of the box. I gasped. I don't know what I had expected to see inside the box; some tiny goblin, perhaps. I know I had not expected to see the enormous goblin *head* that was actually there. That was it—just a head; an ugly head, with green skin, fiery eyes, and a mouthful of ferocious teeth. On its brow sat a golden crown studded with large jewels.

The King's eyes shifted from me to Fauna, then back again. "Where did you find them?" he demanded.

"In the tunnels," said the leader of our group.

"Invaders!" cried the King. "What are you after?"

Before I could think of an answer the old goblin who had been sitting on the steps walked down and stared in my face.

"What is your name?" he asked.

"William."

"William of Toad-in-a-Cage Castle?" he asked in surprise. To *my* surprise, he sounded happy.

I nodded.

"I thought so!" he cried in delight.

"William?" roared a voice from my left. *"William?"*

I turned and shouted out in joy. Igor was here! My joy turned to despair as I realized that he was bound in heavy chains, and that the reason I hadn't seen him before was that he was surrounded by goblins who were tormenting him.

"Igor!" I cried, starting to move toward him. The goblin behind me yanked the rope that was tied around my wrists and pulled me back.

Before I could think what to do next Borg, the old goblin who had been talking to me, ran up the steps and gave the King's box a sharp rap. "This is William of Toad-in-a-Cage Castle!" he cried excitedly. "*Our* William!"

"William of Toad-in-a-Cage Castle?" cried the King in astonishment. "The liberator of the goblins? The hero of the goblin race? The only human we are going to allow to live after the war?"

"The same!" said Borg.

"Welcome, William!" roared the King in a voice that could be heard from one end of the room to the other. "Welcome to Castle Nilbog. Come, you goblins, and welcome the boy who freed you from your prison!"

With a shout goblins came running from all directions.

"No-o-o-o-o!" cried Igor. He began thrashing wildly, trying to break his chains. I wanted to run to him, reassure him that I had not released the goblins on purpose. But before I could move a step a dozen goblins had lifted me to their shoulders and begun marching around the hall chanting, "William! William! The hero of the goblins!"

I twisted to look behind me. The goblins had overcome Igor. Like me, he had been lifted to their shoulders. Unlike me, he was being carried from the room. He was no longer struggling. A moment later our paths crossed.

"Igor!" I cried. "It's not like you think!"

My voice was lost in the tumult of the cheering goblins.

Igor stared at me as he was carried past.

The sorrow in his eyes nearly broke my heart.

## CHAPTER SEVENTEEN
# AT THE GOBLIN BANQUET

After they finished celebrating the discovery of their "hero" the goblins carried me to a large room. It had a cozy four-poster bed, some wooden chairs, and a large wardrobe. Against one wall stood a stone basin through which sweet water flowed without stopping. Bed, chairs, wardrobe, and basin were all carved with either goblin faces or pictures from the forest. Metal sconces mounted on the wall held large clumps of the glowing fungus. The sconces had hoods you could pull around them to darken the room.

The place had a friendly look, and I remembered what Granny Pinchbottom had said about the goblins being household helpers.

On the far wall was a large window that looked out over the city. I crossed to study the view and was surprised to find that the window had no glass. Then I realized that there was no need for glass, since down here there was no wind or rain. (Later I learned that the temperature always stayed the same, too.)

While I was looking out the window the old goblin named Borg came through my door. "William!" he cried cheerfully. "I hope you like it here!"

It was clear he was trying to be nice to me. I was in no mood for it.

"Where are my friends?" I demanded.

"What friends?"

I decided to work my way up in terms of trouble. "Let's start with Herky, the little goblin who was traveling with me."

A puzzled looked wrinkled Borg's rounded orange features. "I've never heard of a goblin named Herky. Of course, I wasn't able to keep track of all the young ones, even before the trouble. I'll try to find out for you."

That sounded encouraging.

"How about Fauna? That's the girl who was with me.

Borg looked more serious this time. "She is not a goblin friend. The fact that she was with *you* has saved

145

her life, at least for now. But she is not a goblin friend."

"Where is she?"

He shook his head. "You don't need to know."

"What about Igor?"

A look of fury crossed Borg's face, and he spit on the floor. "Igor is our enemy! Igor is bad, bad, bad!"

"Igor is my friend," I said firmly.

The old goblin shuffled over and stood right in front of me. He was about a head shorter than I was. He looked up, stared me straight in the eye, and tapped my nose with a long orange finger. "You can be Igor's friend, or you can be the hero of the goblins. You cannot be both. If you are smart, you will be the hero of the goblins, because if you are Igor's friend, you will have to go into the dungeons with him. Then, after a while, you will be dead.

"The goblins are furious, William. They are furious at all human beings except you, because you are the one who freed them from their prison. Everyone is going to suffer, William. Everyone except you. Now, what will you be? Igor's friend—or the friend of the goblins?"

Is it fair to make someone choose like that? I didn't think so. I made a decision. I decided I would have better luck trying to get Igor free if I stayed free myself.

"I'll be the goblins' friend," I said. Something seemed to freeze inside me as I spoke. It's not easy to say what is not true, what is not true for your heart. I felt sick.

Borg nodded. "You are a smart boy." For a moment I wondered if he had read my mind. "Let's sit down," he continued.

Actually, I wanted him to go. I wanted to get the cloak and the collar out of my shirt and hide them someplace. I felt nervous around Borg. His eyes were wise and knowing, and I was afraid he might figure out what I was up to.

"I am counselor to the King," said Borg, settling himself on one of the wooden chairs. "I am also one of the Ten Oldest Goblins. I have seen much, William. I have done much. I am an angry goblin."

I sat in the chair opposite him.

Borg told me many things over the next three "days." He told me about life underground. He told me about goblin society. And he told me about The Time of Troubles, which was what the goblins called the time from about a year before the Baron's grandfather had trapped them in the tower until the night I released them.

The current time they referred to as The Time of Revenge.

"It was hard to understand, William," said Borg, sitting across from me, his wise old face lit only by the fungal lamps. "For as long as we could remember, people had either ignored us or been glad we were around, despite our little jokes. We like to help. We like to tease. That's how we were made. Then for some reason people began to grow angry over our jokes. It was as if someone was stirring up trouble against us.

"One night our friend Igor brought us a message from the old Baron inviting all of the goblins of Nilbog to Toad-in-a-Cage Castle for a celebration. He said it was going to be a peace party. He lied. It was a trap. When the Baron and his wizard lit fires all around we knew there was trouble. Goblins don't like hot fires; we like the cold glow of our fungus. Within seconds a ring of fire surrounded the castle and all the land around it. We had no place to run.

"Then the Baron and his wizard cast their spell. Can you imagine what it's like to feel your spirit being sucked out of your body, sucked out and drawn into a huge, empty place?"

"The place behind the tower door," I whispered.

Borg frowned. "We stayed there for one hundred and twenty-one years, William."

I shivered. I had only been there about ten minutes, and it was the worst memory of my life.

"For the first ten years we mourned and moaned," continued Borg. "For the second ten years we said we would give a reward to anyone who rescued us. For the next ten years we said we would destroy the world if we got out.

"After that, we just went crazy.

"One thing gave us hope. Every eleven years, on Halloween night, we could feel the strength of the spell that sealed the door wane. We knew if we ever got out, it would be at this time. So every eleven years we called and cried for someone to open the door. But no one ever came. No one seemed to understand. No one heard our call.

"Until you. We had ways of seeing into the castle, and we watched you from our prison. We knew you were the one. We called you, and you came! You set us free! That is why the goblins will love you forever, William. But you are the only one. No one else ever came. No one else ever helped us. They left us alone in the darkness for over a hundred years, and now they have to pay!"

• • •

Nilbog had no day or night, yet there were times when the castle grew quiet and most of the goblins rested. Then I would slip into the cloak of invisibility and search for Igor and Fauna.

Each time I did this I traveled deeper into the castle, which seemed to extend as far into the rocky island where it was built as Toad-in-a-Cage Castle extended into the ground beneath it.

I found strange and frightening things: huge, ancient statues that didn't seem as if they had been made by goblins at all; a room filled with bones; a room that had no floor, only a raging whirlpool twenty feet below the door. One night I came across the skeleton of a giant lizard.

I found these things. But I could not find my friends.

I heard things, too. Whenever I paused, invisible, outside a room where goblins were awake, I could hear them talking softly about the war to come, and about their anger with the outside world. Often they were making spears and arrows.

Though the goblins treated me well, the talk of war made me nervous. If I did not succeed in my mission, who knew what might happen?

I began to wear the cloak and collar under my shirt again for fear the goblins might search my room some-time when I was not in it.

In addition to searching for Igor and Fauna, I was looking for the King's body. I wasn't sure it existed, but I figured if you could have a head without a body, you could have a body without a head. I also knew there was no way to put the collar around the King's neck unless I could *find* his neck, which I assumed was attached to his body.

I found it on the fourth "night" of my stay in Nilbog. Hidden by the cloak of invisibility, I was exploring the halls above the main floor. I felt bolder now that I had done this a few times, now that goblins had walked right past me without any sign of seeing me. Quiet was important, of course, and sneezes were always a danger, since I had caught a bit of a cold from the drenching I got on the first part of our trip. But overall I was feeling fairly confident.

The books I had read in the Baron's library made me expect that places would be guarded, but in Nilbog that wasn't so. This confused me until I real-ized that the goblins didn't think there was much to guard things from. They trusted one another, and it

152

was unlikely that any enemies from the surface world would actually find their way down here.

Anyway, I had found one of the seven towers. At the top of the stairs was a thick wooden door that swung open easily, revealing a large room. On the far side of the room a big round window looked out on the glowing city of Nilbog.

In the center of the room was a large bed with a golden cover.

On the center of the bed lay the headless body of the King.

Well. I knew where his body was. I knew where his head was. The only problem was, they weren't anywhere near each other. The body was too big to take to the head, which left only one option: I would have to steal the King's head and bring it to his body.

I planned to visit the Throne Room the next night to see what it would take to kidnap the King's head. But the goblins had other plans: They were going to throw a banquet in my honor.

All the important goblins were invited. Of course, no one had nice clothes anymore, because so much had decayed during the hundred and twenty-one years that the goblins were gone. Much in Nilbog had gone untended then. Borg had told me that the reason some places in the city were dark was that the glow fungus had died. In other places it had grown out of control, covering entire buildings, and the goblins were still cutting it back.

That night the goblins gathered in the great hall of the castle at long stone tables covered with glowing green cloths. I sat at the head table. Karl had told me that was the name of the table where the guest of honor sits. But I was *really* at the head table, because that was what was next to me: the King's head.

All through the meal I kept looking at it, wondering how I could steal it. I was tempted to ask the King how he had gotten that way, only it didn't seem like the kind of thing you asked a king at dinner.

Two young goblins were assigned to take care of the King. They fed him and wiped his mouth, and when he wasn't looking they made silly faces and generally acted up. They reminded me of Herky, and I wondered what had happened to him.

"Eat up, William!" cried the King every five minutes or so. I would smile and nod and chase some food around my plate. But since it was mostly things like boiled lizard tails or fried fungus glop (that wasn't the real name of it, but it's the best way to describe it), I wasn't eager to stuff any of it into my mouth. I don't think dinner should glow in the dark.

Borg sat on the other side of me, pointing out important goblins and telling me hilarious stories about jokes they had played on humans back before The Time of Troubles. I had a feeling that one way you got to be an important goblin was by pulling off a really major joke. I liked the idea. It was better than getting promotions for winning wars.

Only now the goblins had traded in their jokes and were going to war themselves.

When the meal ended someone banged a huge gong for silence. It took a while for the room to quiet down, and we had to wait for three or four food fights to be settled before the King could really talk.

"Goblins of Nilbog!" he cried. "How glad I am to gargle your eyes! War is coming, and we shall splat the bongus of our enemies. Death shall be our uncle's sister. Our victory shall glow in the dark like beezlenuts."

He went on, getting crazier and crazier. He talked about how wonderful the goblins were, how wonderful he was, how wonderful I was, and how wonderful the war was going to be.

The goblins cheered like crazy.

"And now," cried the King, "now it is time to see our greatest enemy!"

The gong sounded again. The great doors at the end of the room swung open, and five huge goblins pulled an enormous wooden cart into the room. I felt as if someone had poured ice into my heart. On top of the cart was a wooden structure: two posts with a crossbar. Chained to the crossbar was Igor.

When the goblins saw him they began to hiss and shout. "Igor!" they screamed. "The enemy, the enemy! Igor, Igor, Igor!" Then they started throwing things at him.

Igor didn't say a word. His head hung down so far that his great black beard drooped beyond his knees. As the cart rolled toward the head table the goblins continued to jeer and shout. Pieces of lizard, bits of fungus, even plates and cups flew through the air, striking his head and back.

Finally I could stand it no longer. Sweeping my arm across the table so that my dishes went clattering to the floor, I climbed onto my chair and then onto the table.

"Stop it!" I cried. "Stop it right now! Igor is my *friend*!"

156

# CHAPTER EIGHTEEN

# OUT OF THE DARKNESS

I had a lot of time to think about what I had done at the banquet, and I didn't regret it.

Well, I did in a way, since it looked as if I was going to die and the goblins were going to launch an all-out attack on the world above. Still, the look on Igor's face when I had announced to the assembled goblins that I was his friend—that had been worth a lot.

I didn't have much time to enjoy it. The King went berserk and started screaming and yelling so hard that his head rolled out of the box and came snapping at my ankles. Borg grabbed my other ankle and tried to pull me off the table. Igor, roaring in rage at the goblins trying to hurt me, pulled his chains so hard that he snapped the wooden beams they were connected to.

It was thrilling to watch him spin around, making the chains and beams swing in a big circle that sent the goblins trying to attack him flying in all directions.

"Leave him alone!" I had cried, leaping off the table. "He's my friend! My *friend*!"

"William Igor's friend!" he roared, trying to battle his way toward me.

But there had been several hundred goblins and only two of us. So now Igor was in a cell somewhere, and I was in a cell as well, no longer the hero of the goblins, no longer living in one of the best rooms in Goblin Castle, merely a prisoner locked in the dark. At least I still had the cloak and the collar hidden under my shirt—though at the moment the amulet would have been more useful.

Time went on. I began to wonder how long I had been there and how long I had to live. I called out to Igor and Fauna, but they didn't answer.

I don't know how long I had lain in the darkness when I heard footsteps coming in my direction. They stopped outside my cell. Had the goblins come to kill me?

A squeak, then a tiny sliver of green light near

the floor. Something blocked it. A scraping sound, another squeak, and then footsteps going away.

After a moment I crawled to where the light had been. I found two metal bowls, one holding water, the other food. The food was probably disgusting, but at least it didn't glow. I ate it, glad, for a moment, of the darkness.


I began to count how often food and water were brought—though since I didn't know how many meals a day they were giving me, I still didn't know how much time had actually passed.

Shortly after the tenth meal I was lying in the darkness, counting my sneezes and wondering what had happened to my friends, when I heard the little door through which food was delivered swing open again.

What was going on? It was only a short time since my last meal—much too early for the goblins to be returning.

I heard a slight noise off to the right. Before I could move, something jumped onto my stomach and whispered, "William!"

"*Herky!*"

"Shhh-h-h-hh! Don't be loud, William. Just be happy."

"Herky, where have you been?"

"Herky bad!" he said fiercely. "Herky been bad to William. Now Herky been bad to goblins. Herky feel funny. Herky feel sad. Herky brought key."

"You brought the key?" I hissed.

"Herky brought three things. Hold out hands."

When I did as he said he placed something cold and metallic in my cupped hands. After a minute it began to glow.

*"The amulet!"* I whispered. "How did you get it?"

"Went back for it. Long way. Got lost once . . . twice . . . three times. But got it, got it for friend William, because Herky was such a bad little goblin."

I had been in the dark so long that the amulet's glow hurt my eyes. I cupped my hands around it to contain the light. "Thank you," I whispered.

"Herky good?" he asked desperately.

I could see his funny little face in the light that leaked from between my fingers. He looked troubled.

"Herky very good," I said sincerely.

He smiled. Then he pulled my hair. "Herky bad!" he whispered fiercely. "Come on, butterhead William— let's go."

"You said you brought three things."

"Don't be bad. Let's go."

With that he squeezed through the little door.

160

For a moment I panicked, until I heard him inserting the key in the lock.

Raising the amulet, I took a look around my cell; four stone walls, a stone bed, and a hole in the corner for relieving myself. I would be glad to be out of here.

"William!" hissed Herky. "Open door!"

I pulled open the door. Herky jumped from the handle to my leg.

In the corridor, directly opposite the door, sat the third thing he had brought.

"Igor's bear!" I whispered in delight.

"Herky good bad good bad," he replied, sounding miserable and happy at the same time.

"Herky good!" I said fiercely, lifting him up and giving him a hug.

"Yuck! Bad William."

But when I put him down he was smiling.

I tucked the amulet inside my shirt, where it continued to glow, but was muted enough that it didn't announce our presence so brightly. It hung above the cloak of invisibility and the golden collar. I picked up the bear.

"Do you know where Fauna is?" I asked Herky.

Herky made a face. "Girl mean!"

"She got your tail out of that rock."

161

He sighed. "Come on, William. We get Fauna. Then we get out of here."

I stopped. Normally I would have waited to explain what else I wanted to do. But my days in the dark had given me time to think. One thing I had thought about was how much sorrow it would have saved Igor if I had told him right at the beginning that I was the one who had let the goblins loose. I had decided life would be easier if I could start getting things out in the open.

"Herky, we have to talk."

He sighed again. "Talk, talk, talk."

"We have to get someone else."

His eyes went wide as he guessed who I meant. "Oh, no. Herky not *that* bad!"

"Herky, Igor is my friend. I know the goblins are mad at him, but what happened is not his fault. He was being used. That old Baron and his wizard—they're the ones to blame."

Herky folded his arms. "No Igor!" he said firmly.

After fifteen minutes I couldn't tell if Herky even knew where Igor was. I suspected he did; it was easy for a little goblin to go almost anywhere in the castle without being noticed, and who knew what those big ears had heard? But he wouldn't say anything but "No Igor!"

Finally I changed my plan. I decided we would get Fauna and then collar the King. If *that* worked, maybe everything else would calm down enough so that we could get Igor loose, too. If not, I didn't know what I would do. I just knew I wasn't leaving Nilbog without my friend.

Fauna's cell was a long way from mine. To my relief, the key that opened my cell worked on hers as well. I decided that, as with the guard situation, the goblins had probably never had enough enemies to worry about escape-proof dungeons.

She was pale and thin-looking but seemed to be all right otherwise. "Thank you," she said when we opened the door. "I thought I might not ever get out of here."

For her, it was a real emotional outburst.

It was time to go collar the King. But I realized I had never had a chance to tell Fauna the things Granny Pinchbottom had told me—partly because I had not wanted to say them in front of Herky.

"We have to talk," I said.

Her cell seemed as safe a place as any, so we stayed there while I repeated everything Granny Pinchbottom had told me.

"Huh!" said Fauna. "I don't like that much. But if Granny Pinchbottom says it's so, I'll believe her."

Herky looked nervous. "Hurt King?" he asked.

"Actually, I think he'll feel much better if we do this. Will you help us?"

He put both his hands in his mouth and nodded.

Even though I warned them what was about to happen, Herky and Fauna made very satisfactory gasps when I slipped into the cloak and disappeared. To my surprise, one thing did not disappear: the glow of the amulet. Fearing it would attract attention, even tucked under my shirt, I handed it to Fauna. The moment it left my hand it faded.

We were at the base of a little-used stair that led to the main floor of the castle. I was to go ahead and signal the others when it was safe to follow. By moving from spot to spot this way we hoped the three of us could stay together.

As I climbed the stair it occurred to me that it might have been smarter to try to collar the King first and then get Fauna. But something about that idea felt wrong.

I paused at the top of the stairs. No one in sight. Though I had totally lost track of time while I was in my cell, Herky had said that it was the castle's quiet time.

I turned and gestured to the others. They ignored me. I couldn't figure out why until I remembered I was invisible. Throwing back the hood, I gestured again.

Herky and Fauna joined me at the top of the steps.

The brass sconces in the hallway had been pulled nearly shut, dimming the fungal glow so that the hall was like a night with no moon, only stars. Raising my hood again, I put a finger to my lips—an unseen gesture, I immediately realized—and started down the hall. Soon I found an alcove with a statue of a former Goblin King—a good place for Herky and Fauna to take shelter if necessary. I looked around. The hall was empty. Throwing back the hood, I gestured for them to join me.

Traveling in this manner, we made it most of the way to the Throne Room. The trip was complicated by the fact that goblin corridors don't run straight but curve and twist in odd ways that make it hard to see very far ahead.

It was the singing that let me know we had a problem. Fauna and Herky were walking toward me when I heard it. Three goblins, from the sound of it, and not far off. I looked back. Herky and Fauna were about twenty feet away.

The goblins were getting closer fast. If they came around the corner before my friends made it to the next safe spot, we were in big trouble.

I had an idea. Without any real sense of whether or not it would work, I ran toward Fauna.

The goblins rounded the corner just as I reached her.

# CHAPTER NINETEEN
# TRYING TO GET A HEAD

Since I was invisible, Fauna didn't realize I was coming back until I was next to her, whispering, "Don't say a word!" Flinging out the edge of my cloak, I drew her in with me.

To my relief, she disappeared instantly.

"This way," I whispered, pulling her toward the wall.

"William, what—"

She broke off when she heard the singing. Though it was hard to move with both of us wrapped in the cape, we managed it. With the two of us invisible, Herky scrambled several feet away, flopped onto his back, and pretended to be asleep.

The three goblins came down the corridor arm

in arm in arm, singing about what they were going to do when the war started. "Wait!" cried one of them. Then he pulled his nose and farted, which made the other two laugh so hard that one of them fell onto the floor.

I held my breath, trying to remain totally silent—though the way they were laughing, I don't think they would have heard me if I had sneezed, which I was trying desperately not to do.

Then they spotted Herky. "Let's play catch!" said one of them, stooping down to pick him up. But the other two had already started on down the hall, so he left Herky and hurried to catch up with them.

When we reached the Throne Room Herky stayed outside to keep watch. Fauna came in with me, because it would be easier to hide inside the room.

Inside I handed Igor's bear to Fauna. Alone, wrapped in the cloak of invisibility, I began the long walk to the throne. A pair of goblins sat on either side of the throne. I wondered if they always guarded the King, even when they thought there were no enemies around, or if they were nervous now that there really were enemies in the castle. It didn't make that much difference; both guards were snoring soundly.

The sounds coming from the wooden box indicated that the King was snoring, too. Hardly daring to breathe, I climbed the four steps to the throne, reached forward, and grasped the handle on top of the King's box. I lifted it as gently as I could, expecting him to scream for help at any moment.

He continued to snore as I headed for the door.

I made it most of the way before I sneezed.

"Gesundheit!" said the box. Then, after a moment of silence, it shouted, "Who sneezed that sneeze? What's going on out there?"

"Shhhh!" I whispered. "It's nothing. Go back to sleep."

"I don't want to go to sleep! I want to know what's going on. Guards! *Guards!*"

With a snort the guards lurched to their feet. They were the biggest goblins I had seen yet, both at least two feet taller than me.

They looked around, uncertain of what was going on.

"Here!" screeched the King. "I'm here!"

I slipped the box inside my cloak. It vanished at once.

Unfortunately, unseen is not the same as unheard.

"Over here, you morons!" screamed the King.

The guards looked more puzzled than before.

"Where are you?" cried one of them.

"Over here!" I shouted, running to the left. Then I turned and ran to the right. "No, I'm over here!"

"Get him!" cried the guards. They ran in circles, bumped into each other, and fell down.

I raced for the door. "Let's get out of here," I hissed to Fauna.

Just when I thought we might make it out without her being seen, the King gave another shout. The guards glanced in our direction, spotted Fauna, and the chase was on.

"Herky!" I shouted as we raced out the door. "This way!" Then, realizing that neither he nor Fauna would be able to follow me if I was invisible, I slipped back the hood.

We had to run down two long, twisting corridors to get to the tower that held the King's body. We had a good start on the guards because of their initial confusion, but they were bigger than we were and gaining fast.

"Help!" cried the King. "Thieves! And washerwomen!"

"Stop!" cried the guards, their voices uncomfortably close. "Stop, you king stealers!"

"This way," I gasped, turning a sharp right. The

guards were close behind when we reached the arch that led to the tower stair.

"Ouch!" cried the King as I started up it. "That hurts!"

I realized his head was bouncing with every step I took. "Sorry," I kept saying. "Sorry, sorry."

We had climbed about twenty steps when the guards arrived. I began to move even faster. Around and around the spiral stair we raced. The King continued to complain. Fauna was silent except for an occasional shout of "Faster!"

Panting, gasping, feeling like I was about to die, I burst into the King's bedchamber. Fauna was inches behind me. I didn't have to say a word to her. Together we grabbed the great wooden door and slammed it shut. As we were lowering the thick bar that would hold it closed the guards arrived. They threw themselves against the door, but it was too late. The bar was in place.

"Where's Herky?" I cried to Fauna. "What happened to him?"

"I don't know. He was with us until we reached the stair. That was the last I saw of him."

"Open up!" cried the guards, pounding on the door.

No time now to try to figure out what had happened

to Herky. I opened the box. The King's head rolled out and bit me on the foot.

"What have you done who are you why are you doing this you stupid boy?" he screamed.

"I'm trying to help!"

"You can't help! You are the goblins' enemy!"

"Sometimes it's hard to tell your friends from your enemies," I said as I opened my shirt. I had to shout to be heard above the banging at the door.

"We have no friends!" screamed the King, foam flying from his mouth. "Apples are eating my feet and everyone has betrayed us. Everyone will pay!"

I reached for his head. "I'm going to try to put you back together."

The head rolled from side to side, trying to bite me.

"Fauna, help me!" I cried.

She had tossed the bear onto the bed and begun pushing things in front of the door, which was already bulging under the repeated blows of the enormous guards. "What do you want?" she asked, crossing to join me.

"I've got to get his head onto the bed. Either that or get his body down here."

She glanced at the King's body, which lay in perfect repose on the golden cover. It was very big. "Head to bed," she said, and the two of us tried to grab it.

But the King was in a frenzy, bouncing, rolling, grabbing whatever he could with his teeth. Finally I tore off my shirt and threw it on top of him. Fauna grabbed the sleeves and hauled him onto the bed.

"Try to get him in place," I said as I began to unbuckle the collar. To my astonishment, I realized I didn't want to take it off. Something about wearing it felt very good.

"William, what are you waiting for?" cried Fauna.

I heard the door begin to crack.

My fumbling fingers seemed awkward as sausages. The King was no longer shouting words, just sounds that had no meaning. Suddenly he sank his teeth into Fauna's hand.

"Ouch!" she cried, yanking her hand away. The King's teeth were still embedded in her flesh, so his head went with her hand. Suddenly it came loose, flying across the room and crashing into a wall. It fell to the floor and bounced twice. When it stopped the King was silent.

"Is he dead?" I whispered in horror.

"I hope not," said Fauna, scrambling off the bed.

She grabbed the head and climbed back onto the bed. With no resistance from the King she easily put it in place on his neck.

A board in the door splintered. A green fist reached through the opening.

Seeing the King's head and body together, I knew he needed the collar far more than I did. Finally I managed to unbuckle it. Holding it before me, I started toward the bed.

I was stopped by a blinding flash of light.

## CHAPTER TWENTY

# HEAD TO HEART

"Take one more step and I'll turn you into a toad," said a familiar voice.

"Ishmael! What are you doing here?"

"Don't call me that!" cried the old magician, shaking his long white beard in distress. "Now put down that collar."

I looked at him in surprise. "Why?"

"Because what you are about to do is both dangerous and stupid. Put it down."

Another board in the door splintered. The babble outside indicated that more goblins had arrived.

I glanced at the collar. "Granny Pinchbottom said this was the only way to heal the King."

Ishmael's bushy eyebrows formed a pair of arches. "You *believed* that wretched old woman?" he asked in astonishment.

As a matter of fact, I had. Though when I thought about it, what she had told me—that the goblins were basically good and helpful—was pretty strange, given everything I had seen.

"William, listen. I made a huge mistake when I met you in Igor's cell a few days ago; I didn't realize who you were. That happens to me a lot these days—my memory is fading. The message I brought for Igor should really have gone to you. 'The most dangerous night' was the night the goblins were likely to break free—the night the spell would be weakest and you would be most vulnerable. I tried to warn the Baron, but he's a fool. Not like his grandfather, may he rest in peace."

The shouting at the door grew louder. Ishmael turned and waved his hands. "Stop that pounding!" he screamed.

To my astonishment, it stopped.

"How did you do that?" I asked.

"Do what?"

I didn't want to start one of his circular conversations. "Never mind. Tell me about the most dangerous night."

"William," said Fauna, "I don't think I like this man."

I didn't want to get involved in that conversation, either. I needed information. Should I put the collar on the King or not? Where was the truth in all this? Who was lying to me?

At that moment the King woke up. "You!" he screamed when he saw Ishmael. "What are you doing here? Help, murder, fire, destruction! Guards, guards, guards!"

"Quiet!" said Ishmael, waving his hand at the King.

The King's eyes went wide. His lips closed and stayed closed, though his cheeks bellowed and expanded as if he was trying to scream something out.

"Tell me!" I said urgently.

I heard a murmur in the hall, as if the spell holding the guards was beginning to weaken.

"Long ago the goblins were running rampant over the countryside, causing chaos everywhere," said Ishmael. "Nothing could be settled, nothing could be calm, nothing could be quiet while they were around. It was like having too many children."

I stared at him in amazement.

"Finally the Baron called me in. He was a good man—quiet, solid, stern. He knew something had to be done about the madness of the goblins, so he asked for my help. Together we spent a year and a day poring through old volumes until we found the key to locking away the goblins. We spent another year and a day preparing the spell. When all was in readiness we sent Igor to the goblins with a message inviting them to the castle for a conference. Igor and the goblins had been friendly, and the poor fool never understood our real plan. Of course, I also used a little magic to help keep him confused.

"On Halloween night the goblins arrived, and the Baron and I put our plan into effect. The silly creatures were so happy to be at the castle, so excited about having a party, that they were completely surprised when the ring of fire surrounded them. Once they were trapped I worked the spell that drew their spirits out of their bodies and imprisoned them in the place we had prepared in the tower."

"And then you cut off my head!" screamed the King, his eyes bulging with rage.

Ishmael looked at his hands and shook his head sadly.

"You know, in the old days that spell would have kept him quiet for hours. I think I need to get more sleep."

"You cut off my head!" screamed the King. "You said you were my friend, and then you cut off my head!"

"Well, you didn't need it anymore. Who thought you would ever be back in your body?" He turned to me. "Cutting off his head put the final seal on the spell. Of course, things that happened to his body while his spirit was out of it didn't affect it the way they normally would have. Anyway, you can see that you cast away years of effort when you opened that door. But it wasn't really your fault. No one had warned you what was there, and I hadn't realized that that meddling fool Granny Pinchbottom was setting you up to break the binding."

I had heard enough. I could tell the goblins were wild and crazy. But if Ishmael thought the kind of lying treachery he was talking about so calmly was better, if he thought Igor and Granny Pinchbottom were fools, if he thought having "too many children" around was a terrible thing, then I decided I would go for the craziness.

Wondering if he really could turn me into a toad, I started toward the bed. At the same moment the goblins outside shook free of the spell and broke down the door.

The result was instant chaos. The goblins—and there were a lot of them now—stumbled over one another as they tried to get through the door. I was trying to reach the King. Ishmael was trying to stop me and hold off the goblins at the same time. Fauna was trying to keep the King's head from rolling off the bed. The King was screaming and trying to bite her.

"Stop it! Stop it, all of you!" cried Ishmael.

I think he was trying to do too much at once. His spell didn't stop me; it simply slowed me down, as if I were in a dream. It did the same to the goblins, who were tumbling toward me, but moving more like feathers than cannonballs.

Ishmael's spell provided time for one more thing to happen as something came from the outside, something that wasn't slowed down by his magic. I heard it first, a deep rumble of a voice coming up the stairs. "William! William, you all right?"

"Igor! Igor, I'm here!"

"See, William?" shouted Herky, bursting through the door. "Bad Herky got Igor for you!"

And then Ishmael's spell came totally undone. I was flying toward the bed, the goblins were flying toward me, and Igor was flying through the door. Landing on the golden cover, I scrambled up the bed. Ignoring the screams of the King, I grabbed the thing Fauna had tossed to the bed earlier and threw it across the room. "Igor!" I shouted. "Catch!"

"Igor's bear!" he cried joyously as he snatched it out of the air. Then he laid into the goblins that were attacking me, crying, "Bop! Bop! Boppity bop bop! You goblins leave that William alone!"

Goblins flew in all directions, bouncing off the walls and screaming with rage. This time they didn't outnumber Igor by hundreds, only by dozens. "Igor happy, William!" he cried as he thrashed about him with the bear.

I didn't have time to answer. As I began to wrap the collar about the King's neck Ishmael snatched the head from the bed. He pulled back his arm. With a shock of horror I realized that he was about to fling the head out the window. I lunged toward him but got tangled in the King's clothing.

"Fauna!" I cried. "Stop him!"

Ishmael released the head. It sailed straight toward the window.

Fauna leapt up and caught it.

With a scream of rage Ishmael raced toward her. Turning, she threw the head toward Igor.

"Bop!" yelled Igor, smacking the head with the

bear and sending it flying back toward me. I grabbed it from the air.

Ishmael turned toward me again, his face twisted with fury. He raised his hands, and I expected to find myself turning into a toad at any moment. But before the old wizard could make another move Herky went bounding through the air and landed on his shoulder. "Bad!" he cried. "Bad, bad!"

Ishmael staggered backwards. With Herky still clinging to his shoulder, he fell through the open window.

"Herky!" I cried in horror.

"Murder, fire, arson!" screamed the King. "Eat the dogs! Kiss your feet good-bye! Die, die, die!"

Fauna scrambled onto the bed, grabbed the King's head by the ears, and placed it firmly on his neck.

I could see tears in her eyes.

Ducking as Igor sent a goblin flying over my head, I wrapped the golden collar around the King's neck. Making sure that head and neck were carefully tucked into the collar, I fastened the buckle.

For a moment it felt as if the entire city was holding its breath. The battle between Igor and the goblins stopped. The only movement was that of Fauna placing her hand on the King's forehead.

Like the city, I held my breath.

"Ishmael bad!" squeaked a familiar voice.

"Herky!" I cried as I saw the little goblin climb back over the windowsill. "How did you get back here?"

"Down bad!" he said. "Jump good! Jump far, grab wall, hold tight."

Fauna smiled. But before she could say anything the King began to move. First his chest began to rise and fall. Then after a moment, he stretched his hands. Lifting his arms, he stared at his fingers, wiggled them—and began to laugh. It was not the laugh of a mad creature. It was a deep, happy laugh, the laugh of someone who has looked at something and found it so good that it fills him with joy.

"Peace," he said to the goblins who filled the room, to Igor, to Fauna, to me. "It's over."

Somehow the city knew it was over, too. Granny Pinchbottom had said that the King and his people had a mystic connection. She must have been right, because we could hear a rising cry of joy and triumph from below.

I crossed to the window to look out at the city. Goblins were flowing out of their buildings, filling the streets, singing, dancing, leaping about with the same wild energy I had seen before. Yet it was different in a way. It took me a moment to realize that what underlay the energy now was not rage but joy.

Herky scrambled onto my shoulder.

Rising from his bed, the King joined us at the window. Fauna came to stand with us, and then Igor, too. The other goblins—the ones who had been fighting Igor but moments before—clustered behind us.

I stared down at the dark water below, wondering if Ishmael had fallen into it or if he had somehow managed to vanish halfway through the fall, returning to wherever it was that he had come from.

The King put his arm around my shoulders. "I name you goblin friend," he said.

Igor put his arm around my shoulders from the other side. "William *Igor* friend," he said.

"Yow!" said Herky, climbing onto my head.

# CHAPTER TWENTY-ONE
# GOBLIN FRIENDS

The return to Toad-in-a-Cage Castle wasn't nearly as difficult as the journey to Nilbog, because the goblins showed us a quick and easy path back to the surface. But not right away. We stayed in Nilbog for another three "days" while the goblins celebrated the King's recovery.

The King declared that Fauna and I were his special friends, and had us moved into rooms right beneath his own. They even gave Fauna her knife back.

Now that Ishmael had admitted that Igor had not known about the plot against the goblins and had been tricked into bringing them to Toad-in-a-Cage Castle, the goblins were willing to forgive my friend for everything that had happened.

It took Igor longer to get used to the idea that the goblins were no longer his enemies than it did them. It finally began to sink in when the two of us took a walk through the streets of Nilbog and several goblins of different sorts gave him cheerful greetings.

Suddenly Igor began to hit himself on the head with his bear. "Now Igor remember!" he cried. "Goblins and Igor used to be friends. Then old Baron told Igor they were bad. Igor got confused. What good? What bad? Goblins seem good to Igor. Baron seem good to Igor. Good Baron say good goblins bad."

"Plus Ishmael used magic to confuse you," I pointed out.

Igor squeezed his bear, which had lost an ear during the battle in the tower. "This all make Igor's head hurt," he said.

The goblins had another feast. This time Herky, Fauna, Igor, and I all sat at the head table, and the King made a speech about how we were Goblin Friends forever.

Later I asked him if the goblins were going to come back out into the world.

"Not right away," he said sadly. "It will take time for us to return. You can't push something out as far as we were pushed and have it come back that easily. But we'll be back. I promise."

One goblin did come back: Herky announced that he wanted to make the journey to the surface with us.

Of all the surprising things that happened after I discovered Igor, I sometimes think the most surprising was the reaction we got when we crossed the drawbridge of Toad-in-a-Cage Castle.

Hulda was the first to see us. "William!" she bellowed, thrusting her round face out of a tower window. "William, you've come home!"

Home? I guess it was home, though I had never really thought that Hulda and the others thought of it as *my* home.

Her joyous cries of greeting brought Karl and the Baron to the windows. Soon they had joined us on the drawbridge—the very drawbridge where the Baron had found me eleven years earlier. It took the better part of an hour to get our story out, and we had to tell it over and over for the next two days, adding details and tying up loose ends.

"Well, that certainly explains a lot," said the Baron over and over. "And I never suspected what grandfather had actually done."

That night Hulda cooked a special dinner, which everyone except Herky enjoyed. It was strange to have Igor at the table with us, and Karl kept glancing at him nervously.

After dinner Karl and I built a huge fire in the sitting room, which was the coziest room in the castle. Then we "adventurers," as the Baron now called us, had to tell our story one more time. Karl made notes. Hulda helped Igor fix the bear's ear.

When we were done the Baron invited Igor, Herky, and Fauna to live in the castle.

"Igor live in castle already," said Igor, sounding puzzled.

"Well, er, I meant *upstairs,* with the rest of us," said the Baron, seeming a little flustered.

"Igor like that," said Igor, giving the Baron a little bop with his bear.

"And how about you, young woman?" asked the Baron.

Fauna shook her head. "It's a very nice offer," she said. "But I already have a home. However, I would like to visit every now and then, if it's all right with you."

"It would be just fine with me!" roared the Baron.

She looked at me questioningly.

"And with me," I said firmly.

She smiled.

Herky was busy cleaning dust out of a corner. "Herky stay, too!" he cried. "Lots to do here. This place good mess!"

Later that night I went to the North Tower. The door hung open, and on the other side I could see—a staircase.

"It changed about a week ago," said Karl, coming up behind me.

I wondered if Ishmael had really died in his fall from the tower. Maybe his magic had vanished with him.

"Have you been up there?" I asked.

He shook his head.

"Let's take a look," I said.

I led the way. The stair curved around and around, opening onto many rooms, all of them perfectly normal looking. I wondered where they had been during the time the tower had been the goblins' prison.

At the top of the stairs was a trapdoor. I lifted it and climbed out. The roof of the tower was flat, surrounded by a low wall.

Overhead the night sky blazed with stars.

Stretching in all directions, as far as I could see, was the world.

I realized that I had barely seen any of it—just a little of what was underneath it.

"Why don't we go out?" I said to Karl. "Why does almost no one come here?"

"I don't know," he said, leaning against the wall and looking out into the darkness. "It was as if the whole castle was locked up somehow, trapped in some strange dream. Things have been different here since the night you let the goblins loose—as if we're waking up."

I smiled.

At a sound behind me I turned and saw Igor, Herky, and Fauna coming to join us.

"Good!" said Herky, climbing onto the edge of the wall and looking out at the world below us.

"Pretty," said Igor, hugging his bear.

"Needs work," said Fauna.

I didn't say anything. Not because I was keeping a secret. Just because sometimes words aren't necessary.

Sometimes being with friends is all you need.

# A NOTE FROM THE AUTHOR

I first met Igor on Halloween night in 1973. I had been a student teacher in a first grade class for the previous two months and the assignment had ended the week before. I was mourning the fact that I would not be sharing my favorite holiday with the kids that I had become so fond of, when Igor . . . *happened.*

He soon became an important part of my life. As a teacher, first in second grade and later in fourth grade, I had to let Igor visit my classroom every year at Halloween. He was always badly behaved, roaring around the room and bopping the kids on the head with his bear. But the kids seemed to love him anyway.

Igor had an aura of mystery about him. Though he was my half-mad twin brother, he was born on Halloween. (My own birthday is in May.) None of us knew how this could be; it just was.

All through the year we would talk about Igor. Sometimes we did Igor math problems. Some of the kids wrote notes to him. He was part of our class-room life.

Finally I decided to write a story about Igor. At first, I thought it would be a picture book. That didn't work. Then I tried a modern story. That didn't work either. Igor, who was said to live in the cellar beneath the cellar beneath the cellar beneath my house, needed a different, older kind of world to rampage around in.

Then one night Igor himself brought me *Goblins in the Castle*. When I asked him where it had come from, who William really was, he was either unable or unwilling to tell me.

That's the way he is.

I took the book to school and read it to my class. It became a Halloween tradition. Sometimes Igor would even read the final chapters when he came for his Halloween visit.

Though I loved the story, fifteen years went by before I found a home for it at Minstrel Books, for which I give great thanks to my editor Pat MacDonald. It was only appropriate that my wife, Katherine Coville, provide the illustrations for the story, as she had had to put up with Igor every Halloween for many, many years.

What is true about this story? That's hard to say.

The only thing I know for sure is that if you try to lock away life's wild energy, sooner or later there will be a price to pay.

As for Igor—well, he's still around, though he appears very rarely these days. Still, if some Halloween night you get a sudden BOP! on the head, don't be too frightened. It's probably only Igor and his bear, out enjoying their favorite holiday.

*Bruce Coville*